先知

中英文經典收藏

紀伯崙——著　謝靜雯——譯

A Bilingual Edition
Gibran's The Prophet

【導讀】

# 不朽的靈魂——紀伯侖

世人總會在紛擾的時刻想起他，追求寧靜時找尋他。他猶如阿拉伯人觀念裡居住在詩人內心、啟示詩句的精靈，為人類的軀殼注入靈魂；又像萬中選一的（al-Mustafa）「先知」，洞悉我們靈性的過去、現在及未來……。

阿拉伯人擁有輝煌的文明，曾在中世紀建立橫跨歐、亞、非三洲的龐大帝國。他們在東西文明的交流與融合上扮演承先啟後的角色，在各領域所達成的偉大成就，至今仍為全世界各民族所享用。

十六世紀初，鄂圖曼土耳其的統治阻礙了他們文明的進程，直至一七九八年，拿破崙的大砲打進埃及領土，才震醒阿拉伯人昏睡已久的覺知，此舉不但開闊了他們的視野，更從此翻開阿拉伯人文嶄新的一頁，堪稱是場「阿拉伯文藝復興運動」。這股風潮從埃及迅速擴散到敘利亞和黎巴嫩地區，有識之士無不關懷國家民族的政治、經濟與文化前途。黎巴嫩詩人、作家、畫家暨思想家紀伯崙（Jibrān Khalīl Jibrān, 1883-1931）便是在這種時代背景與氛圍下誕生。

## 一、紀伯崙的感情世界

紀伯崙出生於北黎巴嫩山區一個貧窮的馬龍教派天主教家庭，這個名喚卜夏里（Bsharri）的鄉村以種植保育類植物——黎巴嫩杉而景色聞名，秀麗純淨的故鄉將最原始的純真注入紀伯崙的血液。

紀伯崙的母親出生於虔誠的天主教家庭，在第一段婚姻裡生下紀伯崙的哥哥，第三段婚姻則生下紀伯崙和兩個胞妹。一八九一年，紀伯崙的父親因職務關係而傾家蕩產，被鄂圖曼政府監禁，直至一八九四年才出獄。

在紀伯侖的記憶中，父親始終是個言語粗暴的醉漢，是與他格格不入的「親人」。他因返回祖國受教育而得以和故鄉的父親重聚，但是他們的相處依舊是兩條歪斜線，毫無交集，直至父親過世，狀況也未曾改善。一八九五年，母親帶著他、哥哥和兩個妹妹移民波士頓定居，父親則獨自留在黎巴嫩。

定居波士頓期間，紀伯侖的母親每天扛著床單、衣服、敘利亞絲挨家挨戶販賣，回家後還得做針線活。兩個妹妹因為傳統思想的束縛而留在家裡幫忙。母親用辛苦攢下的錢協助紀伯侖的哥哥開店，改善家庭經濟狀況。她經常不忍看著年紀僅長紀伯侖六歲的哥哥為全家生計不眠不休的工作，屢次要求紀伯侖幫忙，年少的紀伯侖卻說：「畫家的一根小指頭比得上一千個商人。」或說：「一頁的詩詞，抵得過全世界工廠的紡織品。」就這樣，紀伯侖被這個窮苦的家庭捧在掌心呵護，家人給他充分的愛，他儼然成為家中唯一能夠自在讀書、追夢的閒人。

他對女性的情愫或許就是來自他對母親的愛，以及母親所呈現出來堅毅、慈祥的特質。他認為人類雙唇說出最甜美的話語便是「媽媽」；而女人應該擁有自我，與男人一樣站在太陽底下。母親在紀伯倫的靈魂深處象徵著一切力量的根，而兄弟姊妹的情誼則是紀伯倫對人類的愛與關懷的源。

一九〇三年，紀伯倫從黎巴嫩返回波士頓，當時么妹因肺癆過世，隔年哥哥亦死於肺癆，緊接著，連最愛的母親也因無法承受喪子之痛與病魔的糾纏而撒手人寰，只留下大筆的醫藥債務由他和大妹一肩扛起。這一連串的打擊讓他嚐盡生命的苦澀，然而，苦難的經驗卻成就了他超凡的哲學思想，他以一幅幅的畫作詮釋痛苦與死亡，並且消化它們。我們可以在《先知》中看到他面對「痛苦」的樂觀，以及洞悉「死亡」的豁達：

你的痛苦大多是自己的選擇。

是你內心的醫生用以療癒你病痛自我的苦藥。

信賴那個醫生，緘默平靜地飲下那帖藥方吧：

雖說他下手又重又狠，指引他的卻是上帝溫柔的手，

他端來的藥杯雖然燙灼你的嘴唇，

卻是上帝用祂聖淚滋潤過的泥土所塑造出來的。

什麼是死亡？不就是在風中赤裸佇立、消融於陽光裡？

什麼是停止呼吸？不過是將氣息從騷動不止的潮汐解脫出來，好

讓它升騰擴張、毫無窒礙地追尋上帝？

唯有啜飲靜默之河，你才可能真正歌唱。

唯有抵達山巔，你才可能開始攀登向上。

唯有當大地佔有你的四肢，你才可能真正手舞足蹈。

紀伯崙闡揚愛，但他初次的感情經驗，以及終身不婚的原因，至今仍是個謎。紀伯崙或許曾經歷一段刻骨銘心的愛情，誠如他在《折斷的翅膀》（Al-Ajniḥah al-Mutakassirah）中所描述的女主角莎樂瑪（Salma Karāmah）的境遇，最後他嫁且過世。這位書中的神秘女主角被臆測是紀伯崙返回黎巴嫩求學期間所認識的一位故鄉寡婦，與他的么妹蘇樂坦娜（Sulṭānah）同名。也因此，紀伯崙被稱為「二十世紀的但丁」，兩人皆因熱愛祖國而被放逐；也皆因經歷偉大的愛情而完成不朽之作《折斷的翅膀》和《神曲》。

紀伯崙於一九〇四年結識改變他整個人生的 Mary Haskell 小姐。Haskell 欣賞他的才華，不僅提供物質支助，精神上更成為他的終身摯友。不過由於 Haskell 比他年長十歲，年齡差距成為兩人進一步發展情感的障礙。Haskell 婚後仍持續關懷並支持著紀伯崙。

紀伯崙生命中的女子，還有一位風靡於開羅文壇的黎巴嫩才女麥‧奇亞達（May Ziyādah）。麥於一九一二年寫信給紀伯侖表達對《折斷的翅膀》的讚賞，此後兩人便不時共同探討人生哲理，展開柏拉圖式的心靈交流。他們的信件往返持續至紀伯侖去世前半個月，為期約二十年，後人在這些通信中發現，他倆的關係已從保守的友情進展到親密的書信戀人。紀伯侖的死讓麥受到嚴重打擊，她心理上的創傷始終無法治癒，最終卒於開羅。

紀伯侖的朋友麥卡伊勒（Maykhā'īl Nu'aymah）在《紀伯侖傳》（Jibrān Khalīl Jibrān）中提及，紀伯侖在美國尚有其他不為人知的秘密感情，不過許多將紀伯侖尊為愛與美化身的仰慕者，卻寧可將之斥為謠言。

或許，誠如紀伯侖在《掘墓人》（Haffār al-Qubūr）裡藉魔鬼之口所言：「結婚代表人類被持續的力量所奴役。」因此他選擇不被奴役；我們也能從他所詮釋的夫妻相處之道，來理解他如何重視性靈的獨立：

奉獻你的心，但不要交託給對方保管。

因為唯有生命的手，才能容納你們的心。

你們站在一起，但不要靠得太近；

聖殿的柱子是各自頂立，櫟樹與絲柏也不會長在彼此的遮蔭裡。

## 二、思想背景

童年的紀伯崙受教於故鄉的神父。他努力學習聖經、阿拉伯文和古敘利亞文，並研讀歷史、文學與科學書籍，自幼便顯露藝術天資。他經常用木炭在牆上作畫，四歲時還曾把一張紙埋進土裡，等著紙長大。

初至美國入學時，紀伯崙被錯誤地註冊為他父親的名字 Khalīl

Jibrān，他雖數度反應卻未被訂正，因此西方人都以 Khalil Gibran 來稱呼他。美國求學之初，老師便發掘出他的繪畫資質，校長甚至請攝影家兼出版商 Fred Holland Day 指導他的藝術創作。Day 除了為其引薦藝文界朋友，也讓年少的他因此闖進藝術圈，開始了書籍封面的設計工作——繪畫的技能成為他日後困頓經濟的生機。他對藝術的看法如同詩文創作的理念：「藝術是要表現出樹的魂，而非描繪樹幹、樹枝或樹葉；藝術是要表現海的良心，而不是掀起泡沫的海浪或擾動寧靜湛藍的海水。」

紀伯倫於一八九八年八月返回祖國，在息柯馬學院（Madrasah al-Ḥikmah）接受阿拉伯文和法文教育。他在同儕之間始終文采洋溢、成績優異，是同學們稱羨的詩人。此間，他研讀的古典書籍包括中世紀伊本・卡勒敦（Ibn Khaldūn）的史書、穆塔納比（al-Mutanabbī）的詩集、伊本・西納（Ibn Sīnā）的哲學思想與蘇菲詩，他的老師是當時貝魯特的詩人與戲劇家。這趟黎巴嫩知識之旅奠定了他的古典阿拉伯語文基礎，他也在作品中透露出阿拉伯傳統學術對他所產生的影響。

自黎巴嫩返回波士頓後，紀伯倫在《移民》（Al-Muhajir）阿拉伯文報紙上刊登名為〈一滴眼淚與一絲微笑〉（Dam'ah wa Ibtisāmah）的作品，並陸續出版詩集、散文及小說，探討自由的真諦與社會問題。文章中尤其抨擊鄂圖曼土耳其的統治，並呼籲找回伊斯蘭的榮耀。他在〈一位天主教詩人給穆斯林的信〉中說道：「我厭惡鄂圖曼帝國，因為我喜歡伊斯蘭及伊斯蘭的偉大，我懷抱著恢復伊斯蘭榮耀的期待。我不愛缺陷，但我愛殘缺者的軀體；我厭惡癱瘓，但我喜愛身障者的肢體。」

在 Haskell 的鼓勵與經濟支援下，紀伯倫於一九〇八年赴巴黎學藝，在著名的藝術學校師承法國雕塑家羅丹。旅居巴黎期間，紀伯倫喜歡駐足羅浮宮，這讓他作品「畫中有詩、詩中有畫」的特質朝向更深的層面扎根。

紀伯崙於一九一一年遷居紐約，寄居於藝術家聚集的老社區，與國際著名藝術家、文人、思想家的切磋往來更為頻繁。他勤奮地投入寫作與繪畫，靠著濃咖啡與香菸的慰藉，走過漫長的創作生涯，以致於日後種下無法痊癒的病根。他陸續出版許多阿拉伯文作品，同時以英文寫作。他於一九一八年出版第一本英文作品《瘋人》（The Madman: His Parables and Poems），文辭簡潔，意涵深遠，展現冥思的哲理與昇華的靈性。隔年，他以阿拉伯文創作《隊伍》（Al-Mawākib），這是一首浪漫主義的哲學性對話長詩，內容揭露人類的虛偽與迷惘，呼籲世人擁抱大自然與純真，同時探討人類社會中諸如愛、幸福、正義、知識、宗教等議題，詩中充滿純淨、自然與冥想的特質，為後來的《先知》揭開序幕。

# 三、《先知》的創作

十九世紀中葉，大敘利亞地區在鄂圖曼土耳其的統治下經濟蕭條且民不聊生，迫使信奉基督宗教的黎巴嫩和敘利亞人紛紛移民美洲，以追求更好的生活品質。他們通常在移民地經商維生，並創辦報章雜誌，彼此互動頻繁，遂形成所謂「移民文學」。旅居北美的文人如紀伯侖、麥卡伊勒等因多居住紐約，深受美國文學影響，而被稱為「北派」，至於旅居中南美洲的文人如夏菲各（Shafīq al-Ma'lūf）、米夏勒（Mīshāl al-Ma'lūf），則作品思想相對保守，被稱為「南派」。南北兩派各自成立「筆會」，同時致力於發行報章雜誌，創作不懈。紀伯侖去世後，北派筆會隨之瓦解。由於北派作品多顯露西方思想，遭到許多阿拉伯文學批評家的詬病，然而這些作品對阿拉伯現代文學的影響力卻遠遠勝於南派。

這些移民北美的阿拉伯文人融合阿拉伯文化與新國度的思想，成為阿拉伯浪漫主義文學的代表。他們掙脫古典主義的理性與束縛，重視愛、談論女人，緬懷快樂時光，以大自然作為模範世界的表徵。他們也描寫痛苦的現實，關注貧窮、疾病、無知等主題，因為他們認為生活應是完美無暇的，一旦現實生活不符合理想的樣貌，便必須為之發聲。「冥想」是他們詮釋宇宙真理和生命意義的方式，也展現為對善惡、不朽、毀滅、生死現象的沉思。他們的作品深具創造力，文筆流暢，意義清晰，擅長使用象徵性辭彙。

《先知》是阿拉伯移民文學的經典，也是紀伯倫思想的精華。紀伯倫在書中化身社會改革家，除了是詩人，更是一位哲學家，字裡行間表達對生命的樂觀與希望。這本書內容敘述先知阿穆斯塔法從居住十二年的城市返回故鄉，臨行前，城中居民向他請益物質與精神生活的看法，以期將真理世代相傳。書中包含二十六個主題，探討人與人之間的關係，闡明「愛」是生命的核心，靈魂渴望掙脫束縛回歸原始，得到完全的自由。書中探討的人生哲理獲得世人的共鳴，被譯為五十餘種語言流傳後世。

紀伯崙年輕時便以阿拉伯文撰述《先知》，數度修改後，最終以英文繕寫而成，在Haskell協助修正下，於一九二三年九月出版。紀伯崙曾於一九一八年與麥談及此書：「我想寫這本書已經想了一千年啦！」數年光陰，他將大量時間投入創作，他曾說：「這本小書耗費了我一輩子的光陰，我要確定書中的每一字、每一句，確實是我所能呈現的最佳狀態。」紀伯崙認為此書是他的「重生」。

《先知》除了受到德國哲學家尼采《查拉圖斯特拉如是說》（*Also sprach Zarathustra*）的影響，也沾染阿拉伯古典文學的色彩。它的內容如同許多中世紀的阿拉伯文故事，以呈現人生哲理為目的，也如同阿拉伯傳統講詞與訓囑，慣常以格言式兼顧音韻和諧的詞句呈現。此外，傳統阿拉伯詩經常以對話、獨白、故事鋪陳，並以帶有哲理的詩句作結的手法，在《先知》中也並不陌生。紀伯崙以簡潔的文辭與意義深邃的哲理作為主體，以思想引導形態，未嘗不是承襲了阿拉伯文學的傳統，因此西方人譽之為「東方的神祕主義」。阿拉伯文藝復興之後，紀伯倫思潮成為一股新的動力，影響遍及阿拉伯現代詩、散文、小說、戲劇、音樂等各種形式與思想內涵。

《先知》出版後，紀伯倫的聲望達到頂峰，然而他的健康狀況卻每況愈下。他於一九三一年死於肺病，遺體被運回故鄉，葬於他生前囑咐妹妹買下的一座七世紀古老修道院，並在當地設立「紀伯倫博物館」展出遺作、遺畫與生前遺物。紀伯倫的墓誌銘是他生前的囑託：「我和你一樣活著。現在我站在你身旁，請你闔上雙眼，轉過來，會看到我就在你眼前。」

的確，我的心靈導師——紀伯倫，伴隨著我走過漫長而崎嶇的人生旅途，從年輕歲月到兩鬢花白，從小島到遙遠沙漠。因為他，在人煙稀少的荒漠裡，我彷彿身懷 Zamzam 聖水，豐盈而滿足；在人群熙攘的小島，我彷如身處深山幽谷，寧靜而自由。

猶記大學二年級時愛上他的阿拉伯散文詩，從欣賞到背誦，每天總有一股莫名的喜悅督促著我親近他。儘管當時不盡瞭解其中深意，卻總感動得淚流滿面或獨自會心的微笑，因為他的聲音能自然而然地觸動所有清純的心靈。年輕的我從此不曾衰老，心靈如同潛入大海一般不斷渴求向下探底，尤其是沈浸在阿拉伯語言、文學，以及豐富的文化底蘊。紀伯侖的文筆儘管清晰明白，但所含藏的深意卻彷如宗教聖典，需要細細地品嚐。有時他短短的一句話，得耗費你一生的時光去體會，然而你一旦理解，便已然擁抱著真理，將之內化為思想的一部分。

多年來，對他的話語，我從懵懵懂懂的附庸風雅到產生銘心刻骨的共鳴。今日，我將閱讀他的作品視為「回歸原始的樸真」，是擁抱母親的溫暖，是面對災難的勇氣，更是掙脫束縛的自由。紀伯侖所賜予我的，是無法捨棄的生命價值，更是古老靈性的呼喚。我時常叮囑學生：「去背誦紀伯侖的文章吧！它不僅能奠定你的阿拉伯文學底子，更重要的是，它會改變你的人生，讓你永遠懷抱著希望與赤子之心。」

本書譯者謝靜雯小姐亦秉持對此書的熱愛著手翻譯，誠如紀伯侖所言，用「從內心抽出的線縷來織布，彷彿你的摯愛就要穿戴那塊布四」的精神，以清麗的文筆，忠實呈現紀伯侖不朽的哲理。而更令人期待的或許是，透過此書的重新出版，紀伯侖詮釋的愛能廣佈在現代社會，讓讀者的心靈有所依託，不再徬徨。

國立政治大學阿拉伯語文學系教授　鄭慧慈

# THE PROPHET

先知　目次

# 船來了

THE
COMING
OF THE
SHIP

受到上蒼揀選與鍾愛的阿穆斯塔法，對他的時代來說宛如啟蒙曙光。他在奧菲里斯城前後等待十二年的光陰，殷殷期盼船隻回來載他返回出生的島嶼。

第十二個年頭，收穫月的第七日，

他登上城外的山丘遠眺海洋，看見他的船乘霧而來。

他的心門霍然開敞，喜悅越過海面飛向遠方。

他合上雙眼，在靈魂的靜默裡禱告。

就在他走下山丘的當兒，哀傷卻襲上心頭。

他在心中默想：

我要如何平靜無憂地離去？

不，離開此城時，我的靈魂勢必帶著傷痕。

我在城牆之中度過漫漫的痛苦白晝，歷經長長的孤寂黑夜。

誰能了無遺憾地向自己的痛苦與孤寂揮別？

我在大街小巷裡撒下了太多心靈碎片；

我有太多渴望，恍如裸身晃蕩的孩兒，遊走穿梭在這些山丘上。

我無法毫無牽掛與痛苦地離開它們。

它不是我今日可以隨手拋開的衣物，而是必須親手剝離的肌膚。

它也不是我可以棄諸腦後的思緒，而是因飢渴而愈發甜美的心。

可是我無法耽擱下去。

召喚萬物的大海，也在召喚我。

我必須登船。

縱使時光在夜裡熒熒燃燒，但如果我留下來，

就意味著會凍結僵固並受困於鑄模之內。

我多希望帶著這裡的一切同行，但我又怎麼能夠？

聲音載不動賜它羽翼的嘴唇與舌頭；聲音只能獨自尋覓天空

老鷹必得離巢而去，才能獨自飛掠太陽。

現在他行至山腳，再次轉身面海。

他看到他的船逐漸駛近港灣，故鄉的水手正佇立在船首。

他的靈魂向他們呼喚，他說：

我古老母親的子孫，你們這些駕馭潮浪的人，

有多少次你們在我的夢裡航行，如今卻在我清醒的時刻到來；

而清醒時分正是我更深沉的夢境。

我已經整裝待發。

我的熱切有如張滿的船帆，只待風起。

只要再讓我呼吸一口沉靜的空氣，

只要再讓我回首拋出眷戀的一瞥。

然後我就會加入你們的行列，成為海員中的海員。

而你，遼闊的大海，沉睡的母親，

獨獨妳能為河川溪流帶來和平與自由，

就讓這條溪流再蜿蜒一回，讓它再一次淙淙流過林間，

然後我就會投入你的懷抱，猶如無限的水滴進入無邊的大海裡。

他走啊走著，遠遠便看到了男男女女離開田野與葡萄園，紛紛朝著城門趨來。他聽見他們叫喚他的名字，在田野間奔相走告船已到的消息。

他對自己說：

離別之日，莫非也是團聚之日？

難道我的日暮，實則是我的黎明？

那些把犁具半路拋在畦溝上的人、中途停下榨酒轉輪的人，

我能給他們什麼？

我的心會不會成為結實纍纍的樹木，供我採摘分贈他們？

我的渴望會不會像噴泉那樣湧流，讓我得以斟滿他們的杯？

我會不會是一把豎琴，讓全能上帝的手可以彈撥？

我會不會是一管橫笛，讓祂可以將氣息吹遍我的身體？

我向來追尋靜默。

我在靜默裡覓得了什麼寶藏，可以信心滿滿地分享出去？

倘若今天正是我的豐收之日，

我過往曾在哪片田野、在哪個不復記憶的季節播下了種子？

如果這真的是我高舉燈籠的時機，燈裡燃燒的絕非我自己的火焰

我舉起的燈籠空蕩漆黑，而夜的守護者會替這燈注油點火。

他將這些話語說出口，但心裡留下更多未說。

因為他無法道出自己更深沉的祕密。

他步入城裡，眾人迎了上來，齊聲向他呼喊。

城裡的長老趨前說道：請不要就這樣離開我們。

你一直是我們薄暮的午陽，你的青春曾經給予我們夢想。

你在我們當中並非外人，更不是過客，而是我們的子弟與摯愛。

請別讓我們的雙眼因為渴慕你的臉而吃盡苦頭。

男祭司與女祭司對他說：

別讓海浪將我們隔離，別任我們共度的歲月盡成追憶。

你如同在我們之間漫步的魂靈，

你的身影有如映照我們臉龐的光亮。

我們愛你至深，但這份愛向來是罩著面紗的無言之愛。

可是此刻，這份愛高聲向你呼喚，坦露在你的面前。

離別在即，才知道愛有多深。

其他人也來懇求他，但他並未答話，兀自垂著頭。

站在附近的人們看到他的淚水垂落胸前。

他偕同人們走向聖殿前方的大廣場。

名叫艾蜜特拉的女人從內殿裡走出來，她是個預言家。

他無比溫柔地看著她，因為當年他才進城一天，她就主動來找他

並全心信任他。

她向他致意：

神的先知，探求至高真理的人，

長久以來你踏遍天涯海角尋覓你的船。

如今你的船已經到來，你必得離開。

你深深嚮往著故土家鄉，那裡充滿回憶，

更是你想落地生根的地方。

我們的愛束縛不了你，我們的需求無法強留你。

但在你離開我們之前，請跟我們談談，將你所知的真理昭示大眾。

我們會傳給後代，而他們也會繼續傳給子孫，使它永不滅散。

你在孤獨中守護我們的白晝；

你在清醒時傾聽我們在睡夢中的哭泣與歡笑。

現在請向我們揭示我們的真貌，

告訴我們你對生死之間的一切領悟。

他回答：

奧菲里斯的人們，除了此刻正在你們靈魂裡湧動的事情，

我還能說些什麼？

# 愛

LOVE

艾蜜特拉接著說，跟我們談談愛。

他抬頭望向眾人，眾人靜默下來。

他用宏亮的聲音說：

當愛向你召喚，跟隨他，雖然他的道途艱險陡峻。

當他展翼擁你入懷，依順他，雖然藏在翼尖的利刺可能會傷害你。

當他對你說話的時候，相信他，雖然他的聲音可能會粉碎你的夢想，猶如北風將花園吹成荒涼。

愛會為你加冕，也會將你釘上十字架。

他會助你成長如樹，也會將你修剪管束。

他會攀升到你的梢頭，輕撫你在陽光中顫動的幼嫩枝條。

他也會垂降到你的根柢，搖撼你緊緊攀附土地的根鬚。

愛會像收割稻穀般地將你採集起來。

他舂打你，讓你渾身赤裸。

他篩濾你，讓你擺脫糠殼。

他碾磨你，使你潔白。

他揉捏你，使你柔順；

接著將你送進聖火，烘烤成為上帝聖餐裡的聖糧。

愛會讓你經歷這些種種，使你領悟自己內心的祕密，

進而成為生命之心的片段。

可是如果你因為恐懼，只顧尋求愛的平安與愛的逸樂，

那麼你不如遮掩自己的赤裸，離開愛的打穀場，

踏入季節不分的世界——

在那裡，你笑不能盡興，哭無法盡情。

愛除了自身，別無所予；愛除了自身，別無所取。

愛不佔有，也不被佔有；因為愛有自己，就已足夠。

你愛的時候，不應該說「上帝在我的心中」，

而應該說「我在上帝的心中」。

別以為自己可以主導愛的方向；

愛如果認為你值得，自然會引導你的方向。

愛除了成就自我之外，別無他求。

可是如果你愛著，必定有所渴望，就讓這些事情成為你的渴望：

融化成為奔流的小溪，對著黑夜吟唱旋律；

體會柔情過多的痛苦；

因為體認到愛而受到傷害；

心甘情願地淌血。

黎明時甦醒，心有如長出翅翼，感謝又有另一天能愛；

正午時歇息，冥想愛的狂喜；

黃昏時返家，心存感激；

入睡時分，在心裡替摯愛禱告，唇間吟誦讚美之歌。

# 婚姻

## MARRIAGE

艾蜜特拉接著開口問到：那麼婚姻呢，大師？

他回答：

你們一同降生，也將終生相守相依。

當死神的白色羽翼驅散你們的生命，你們應當相守。

是的，即使在上帝的靜默回憶裡，你們也應當相依。

可是兩人相處的時候，要在彼此之間留點空隙，

讓蒼穹的風得以在你們之間舞動。

彼此相愛，但不要讓愛成為羈絆：

讓愛成為躍動於你們靈魂海岸之間的汪洋。

盛滿彼此的杯，但不要同飲一杯。

分享彼此的麵包，但不要共食一條。

一同歌唱舞蹈，共享歡愉，但要有獨處的時間，

即使是隨著同一首樂曲顫動，魯特琴的琴弦依然各自獨立。

奉獻你的心，但不要交託給對方保管。

因為唯有生命的手，才能容納你們的心。

你們站在一起，但不要靠得太近：

聖殿的柱子是各自頂立，橡樹與絲柏也不會長在彼此的遮蔭裡。

# 孩子

## CHILDREN

有個女人將孩子摟在胸前，她說，跟我們談談孩子。

他說：

你的孩子並不是你的，他們是生命對自己的渴望所衍生的兒女。

他們經你而生，但不是從你而來，

雖然他們與你同在，但並不屬於你。

你可以給他們愛，但不能給他們思想，

因為他們有自己的思想。

你可以提供居所給他們的身體，而不是他們的靈魂。

因為他們的靈魂棲居於明日之屋裡，你就算在夢中也無緣造訪。

你可以努力仿效他們，但不要逼他們模仿你。

因為生命不會倒退著走，更不會在昨日滯留。

你是一把弓，孩子猶如活箭，從你那裡射發。

弓箭手在無限的路途上看到目標，於是使力彎折你，

好讓祂的箭矢飛得又快又遠。

你就在弓箭手的手裡歡喜甘願地彎折吧。

祂愛疾飛的箭矢，也愛穩健的弓。

# 施予

GIVING

有個富人說，跟我們談談施予。

他回答：

你獻出自己的財物時，給的微不足道。

你給出自己，才是真正的施予。

你的財物是什麼？不正是你害怕明天會需要而儲備守護的東西？

過度謹慎的小狗跟隨朝聖者前往聖城時，沿途把骨頭埋在不留痕跡的沙地裡，明天又能給牠帶來什麼？

對匱乏的恐懼是什麼？其本身不正是一種匱乏？

水井滿溢，你卻害怕口渴，這不正是無法消解的乾渴？

有些人擁有許多，但只將少許奉獻出來——

他們沽名釣譽，暗藏的慾念減損了那些餽贈的美好。

那些擁有不多的人，卻將一切都奉獻出來。

這些人信仰著生命以及生命的豐饒，他們的錢箱永遠不會匱乏。

有些人忍痛施予，而痛苦就是他們的洗禮。

有些人歡喜施予，而喜樂就是他們的回報。

有些人單純地施予，不覺得痛苦，也不為尋求喜樂，

更不會懷著行善的念頭。

他們施予的時候，有如遠處幽谷的長春花向空中吐露芬芳。

上帝透過他們的雙手說話，藉由他們的雙眸笑看大地。

在有人求助時施予固然不錯；

無人開口就心領神會主動施予更好；

對慷慨大量的人來說，

尋找願意接受施予的對象，比施予本身更為快樂。

有什麼是你無法割捨的呢？

你所擁有的一切終將分贈散盡，不如現在就施予。

將施予的時機留給自己，而不是留給你的後人。

你常常說「我願慷慨解囊，但只想給受之無愧的對象」。

你果園裡的樹木不會這麼說，牧草地上的畜群也不會這樣講。

牠們施予，是為了存活；留存不放，就會步上滅亡。

值得上蒼賜予白晝黑夜的人，當然值得你施予的其他一切。

有資格汲飲生命之海的人，就有資格從你的小溪舀滿自己的水杯。

有什麼美德更勝於接受給予的勇氣與信心——甚至是慈悲？

你何德何能，竟要人撕開胸脯、揭開自尊，

好讓你一窺他們赤裸的價值與無所遮掩的尊嚴？

先確定你自己是否配當施予者以及施予的工具吧。

是生命施予生命自身——

自認施予者的你，只不過是見證者。

身為受惠者的你們——你們全是受惠者——無須背負感激的重擔，

免得你將枷鎖套在自己跟施予者的身上。

倒不如將餽贈當成羽翼，隨同施予者乘翅升騰飛翔。

過度在意自己所虧欠的，等於是懷疑施予者的慷慨。

施予者以樂善好施的大地為母，以上帝為父。

# 飲食

EATING
AND
DRINKING

然後有個經營客棧的老人說，跟我們談談飲食。

他說：

願你們可以仰賴大地的香氣生存，如同氣生植物依靠光線維生。

可是，既然你們為了食用而必須殺生，為了解渴而必須向初生羔犢的母親搶奪乳汁，那麼，就讓這事成為敬拜之舉吧。

讓你的餐桌化為祭壇，將森林平原上純潔無邪的動物，獻祭給人類本性裡更純潔無邪的部分。

當你宰殺牲畜的時候，在心裡對牠說：

「屠宰你的這股力量也會屠宰我；我也會被吞食殆盡。

將你送進我手中的法則，也會將我送進更為強大的手裡。

你的血跟我的血，只不過是餵養天國之樹的汁液。」

當你啃咬蘋果的時候，在心裡對蘋果說：

「你的種子將會在我的體內存活，你明日的花苞將會在我的心中綻放，你的芬芳將會成為我的氣息，我們將會一同歡度四季。」

秋季，當你採摘園裡的葡萄來榨酒時，在心裡說：

「我也是座葡萄園，我的果實將會被採摘榨汁，

我也會像新酒一般，被存放於永恆的容器裡。」

冬季，當你取酒的時候，在心裡對著每杯酒唱一首歌；

在樂曲裡謳歌對秋日、葡萄園與榨酒機的回憶。

# 工作

## WORK

接著有位農夫說，跟我們談談工作。

他說道：

你們工作是為了跟上大地，為了與大地的靈魂齊步並進。

遊手好閒就會成為四季的陌生人，脫離生命的行列；

這個行列態度莊嚴、傲然又順服地大步邁向無限。

你們工作的時候，有如一把橫笛，時光的低語透過笛心化為音樂。

你們當中有誰願意成為蘆葦，在他人齊聲同唱的時候，唯獨自己喑啞沉默？

總是有人告訴你們，工作是詛咒，勞動是不幸。

可是我跟你們說，當你們工作的時候，便實現了大地一部份最遼

遠的夢想；在那個夢想萌生之初，這部分就已經指派給你們。

勤於勞動，便是真正熱愛生命，

透過勞動熱愛生命，就會熟知生命最內在的祕密。

可是如果你們在痛苦之中，

將降生視為苦難，將供養肉體視為刻寫在眉梢上的詛咒，

那麼我的回答是，

唯有你們眉梢上的汗水，才能沖刷掉刻寫在上頭的字句。

有人告訴你們，生命是黑暗，

而你們在疲憊之時也附和了疲憊者的話語。

我說，生命的確是黑暗的，除非有衝動。

所有的衝動都是盲目的，除非有知識。

所有的知識都是枉然的，除非有工作。

所有的工作都是空虛的，除非有愛。

當你們懷抱著愛工作，

你就會跟自己、跟彼此、跟上帝緊緊結合相繫。

何謂懷抱著愛工作？

就是用從內心抽出的線縷來織布，彷彿你的摯愛就要穿戴那塊布匹。

就是懷抱深情來建造房屋，彷彿你的摯愛就要住進那間屋宇。

就是以柔情來播種、以喜樂來收割，彷彿你的摯愛就要享用果實。

就是要將你靈魂的氣息，注入你打造的一切。

就是要知道，所有蒙福的故人就站在周圍守望著你。

我常常聽你們彷彿夢囈一般地說：

「雕刻大理石，在石頭裡找出自己靈魂的樣貌，

這種人比耕種土地的人更為高貴，

捕捉虹彩，用它在布帛上織出人的形象，

這種人比替我們雙腳製鞋的人更了不起。」

可是我要說——

我不是在說夢話，而是處於正午神智清明的狀態——

風對巨大櫟樹說話的語調，不會比對渺小草葉更為甜美：

將風聲化為歌曲，以愛使曲子更甜美，這樣的人才了不起。

工作是愛的具體表現。

如果你工作時，懷抱的不是愛而是厭惡，

不如拋下工作，坐在聖殿門口等那些樂於工作的人施捨賙濟。

如果你漠不關心地烘焙麵包，烤出來的苦澀麵包只能讓人半飽。

如果你百般不願地壓榨葡萄，你的不滿就會在酒裡注入毒素。

即使你的歌喉宛如天使，但並不真心喜愛歌唱，

那麼你的歌聲就等於摀住了人們聆聽日夜之聲的耳朵。

# 歡喜與悲傷

## JOY AND SORROW

接著有個女人說，跟我們談談歡喜與悲傷。

他答說：

你的歡喜就是掀開假面的悲傷。

你的歡笑往往從注滿了你淚水的同一口井湧現，

怎麼可能有別的情況？

悲傷在你的存在上刻鑿得越深，你就能容納越多的喜樂。

你用來盛酒的杯子，不就是在陶匠的窯爐裡燒煉過？

撫慰你靈魂的魯特琴，不就是用利刃挖空的木頭？

你歡喜的時候，望進自己的內心深處，

就會發現如今讓你歡喜的，正是當初讓你悲傷的。

你悲傷的時候，再次觀看自己的內心，

就會看出如今使你哭泣的，正是當初使你喜悅的。

你們當中有人說「歡喜勝過悲傷」，有人又說「不，悲傷勝過歡喜。」

可是我要告訴你們，歡喜與悲傷不可分割。

它倆聯袂來到，一個與你同桌用餐之時，

謹記，另一個就在你的床上酣眠。

的確，你就像在悲傷與歡喜之間懸盪的天平。

唯有當你淨空的時候，才能達到靜止平衡。

當看守財物者將你提起來秤量金銀，

你的歡喜或悲傷必定隨著升降起伏。

# 房舍

## HOUSES

接著有個泥水匠趨前說道，跟我們談談房舍。

他答說：

你在城牆之內建造房舍以前，先想像自己在曠野裡打造一座涼亭。

你在暮色降臨時有家可歸，你內心那位遙遠孤獨的漂泊者也應如此。

你的房舍就是你軀體的延伸。

它在陽光下成長，在黑夜的靜止中沉眠；它並不是無夢的。

你的房子難道不會作夢？

難道房子不會夢見自己遠離塵囂城市，前往樹林山間嗎？

但願我能將你們的房子收攏在手裡，然後播種似地撒向森林與草地。

但願你們以山谷為街道，以翠綠小徑為巷弄；

但願你們可以在葡萄園裡探訪彼此，衣裳沾染著土地的芳香。

可是這些事情一時還無法實現。

你們的祖先出於恐懼，讓你們聚居得過度緊密；

而那份恐懼會再延續一段時日。

城牆會暫且繼續分隔你們的住居與田野。

告訴我，奧菲里斯的人們，你們的房子裡有什麼？

你們緊閉門戶，又是為了守護什麼？

你們享有平安嗎？

平安是寧靜動力，可以彰顯你們的力量。

你們享有回憶嗎？

回憶是微亮拱橋，可以橫跨心靈的顛峰。

你們享有美感嗎？

美感可以將心從木石塑造出來的事物，帶往神聖的山巔。

告訴我，你們的房子裡有這些嗎？

還是說你們只有舒適，以及對舒適的渴求。

舒適就是以賓客身分登堂入室，繼而喧賓奪主，

最後成為主宰的鬼祟東西？

對，舒適會變成馴獸師，執起彎鉤跟皮鞭，

將你更大的慾望當成傀儡來操弄。

雖然它雙手如絲，但心如鐵石。

它會哄你入睡，但只會站在床畔譏笑肉體的尊嚴。

它會嘲弄你健全的官能，把它們當成易碎器皿似地擺在薊絨毛當中。

的確，貪圖舒適的慾望會扼殺靈魂的熱情，

然後在送葬隊伍裡咧嘴嬉笑。

可是你們這些空間的孩子啊，

在歇息中蠢動不安，不該受到誘捕或馴服。

你們的房子不該是船錨，而該是桅杆。

房子不該是覆蓋傷口的發亮薄膜，而應該是守護雙眸的眼簾。

你們不該住在逝者替生者建造的墳墓裡。

你們不該為了害怕牆壁塌裂而屏住呼吸。

你們不該為了穿過門口而收斂羽翼，不該為了閃避天花板而低垂腦袋，不該為了害怕牆壁塌裂而屏住呼吸。

縱使你們的房子氣派輝煌，

都存藏不住你們的祕密，也收容不了你們的渴望。

因為你們內心裡的無盡，棲居於蒼穹的華廈裡，

以晨間的霧氣為門，以夜晚的歌曲與闃靜為窗。

# 衣物

## CLOTHES

然後有位織工說，跟我們談談衣物。

他答：

衣物將你們的美遮去了大半，卻掩不住醜。

雖然你們藉由衣物尋求私密的自由，得到的卻是束縛與枷鎖。

但願你們能多以肌膚而非衣衫，迎向陽光與清風。

因為生命的氣息就在陽光裡，生命之手就在風中。

你們有人說，「北風織出了我們身上的衣裳。」

我說，是的，是北風沒錯。

但他把羞愧當成織布機，把織軟的筋腱當作縫線。

當他一完成工作，就在森林裡縱聲大笑。

不要忘記，端莊衿持是用來抵擋不潔目光的盾牌。

當不潔者不復存在，端莊衿持豈不成了心靈的束縛與污垢？

不要忘記，

大地喜愛觸摸你的赤腳，

風兒渴望與你的髮絲嬉戲。

# 買與賣

BUYING
AND
SELLING

有個商人說，跟我們談談買與賣。

他回答：

大地為你們結出果實，

只要你們知道如何盛滿雙手，就不會有所匱乏。

你們藉由交換大地的贈禮，就會得到豐裕與滿足。

但是進行交換時，除非秉持著愛與仁慈公正，

否則只會將某些人帶向貪婪，將其他人帶往飢餓。

在海洋、田野與葡萄園裡勞動的人們，

你們在市集裡跟織工、陶匠、香料採集者相遇的時候——

召喚主宰大地的魂靈來到你們之中，

將秤具與估量物價的方法加以淨化。

別讓不事生產的人加入你們的交易，

他們只會販賣空話來換取你們的勞力。

你們應該對這樣的人說：

「跟我們一起下田耕種，或是隨我們的兄弟一同出海撒網；

因為土地跟海洋對你慷慨大方，就像對我們一樣。」

如果歌者、舞者跟吹笛手也來到市集——

買下他們的天賦贈禮吧。

因為他們也採集了果實與乳香；

儘管他們帶來的東西是以夢想塑造出來的，

卻是你們靈魂的衣飾與食物。

在你們離開市集以前，要確定無人空手而歸。

直到你們當中最卑微的人也得到滿足，

否則主宰大地的靈魂將無法在風中安眠。

# 罪與罰

## CRIME AND PUNISHMENT

接著，城裡有位法官趨前說：跟我們談談罪與罰。

他回答道：

當你的心靈乘風流浪，你在毫無防備的獨處狀況下，對他人做了不義的事，等於也對自己行了不義。

為了自己曾犯下的過錯，你必得在天國大門叩門等候，好一陣子備受冷落。

你的神性自我就像大海，永遠不會受到玷污；

如同大氣，只會幫助擁有羽翼的東西高飛。

你的神性自我有如太陽，

它不清楚鼴鼠的地道，更不會尋覓蟒蛇的穴洞。

但你的存在裡不僅僅有你的神性自我。

你心中有大半是人，另有一大半尚未成人，

而是在迷霧中夢遊、尚未成形的侏儒，

這侏儒正在尋覓自己的甦醒。

現在，我就要談談你內在的那個人。

懂得罪與罰的，是他，而不是你的神性自我，

更不是那個迷霧中的侏儒。

我常常聽你們說起犯錯的人，說得彷彿他並非你們當中的一分子，而是你們之中的陌生人，是擅闖你們世界的不速之客。

可是我要說，即使是聖潔正義之士，

都超越不了你們人人內心的至善。

邪惡軟弱之人，也不會沉淪墮落到比你們內心的極惡還要低下。

唯有在整棵樹默認的情況下，一片葉子才會枯黃。

如果沒有你們全體隱藏的意念，犯錯者不可能為非作歹。

你們就像是一同邁向神性自我的行列。

你們既是道路，也是旅人。

你們當中有人跌倒時，是為了提醒後來者有絆腳石要避開。

是的，他之所以會失足也是因為前方的人。

他們的步履固然更快速更穩健，卻未將絆腳石挪開。

以下這段話雖然會重重壓住你們的心頭——

但遭到殺害的人，對於自己遇害未必毫無責任，遭到搶劫的人，對於自己遭劫未必沒有過失。

正義之士對於壞人的作為並非全然無辜。

清白之士對於罪人的行徑並非全無牽扯。

不過，被定罪的人往往為了未被定罪、未受指責者背負著重擔。

是的，犯罪者通常是受害者的犧牲品。

你無法將正義跟不義、善與惡區分開來；

因為它們並肩站在太陽面前，有如錯綜交織的黑線與白線。

當黑線斷裂的時候，織工不僅會查看整塊布匹，更會檢查織布機。

如果你們當中有任何人要審判不忠的妻子，

請先用天平秤她丈夫的心、先用量尺量測他的靈魂。

想要鞭打犯錯者的人，請先看看受冒犯者的靈魂。

如果你們當中有人要以正義之名來處罰他人，就像用斧頭劈砍邪惡的樹木，動手前請先瞧瞧它的樹根；

的確，他會發現有好根與壞根，能結果子的根與結不出果子的根，全都交纏糾結在大地的沉默之心裡。

想要主持正義的法官啊，

肉體上誠實但心靈上欺盜的人，你們要如何審判？

屠戮他人肉體，自己心靈卻飽受摧殘的人，你們要怎麼懲處？

行為上欺騙壓迫他人，自身卻受到侵害踐踏的人，你們要怎麼控告？

悔恨程度已經超過罪行的人，你要如何懲罰？

悔恨不正是你樂於奉行的法律所要伸張的正義嗎？

可是，你無法將悔恨加諸於無辜者身上，

也無法讓犯罪者的心從悔恨中解脫出來。

悔恨會在午夜不請自來，人們會因此甦醒並凝視自身。

除非把所有的行為攤在燦燦天光下檢視，

不然你要如何瞭解正義？

唯有那時你才會曉得，

正直者與墮落者只不過是同一人，

站在微光朦朧的地帶，

介於侏儒自我的黑夜以及神性自我的白晝之間。

聖殿的房角石，並不比地基最底層的礎石更高。

# 法律

## LAWS

接著有位律師說，我們的法律又如何，大師？

他回答：

你們喜歡制訂法律，可是卻更喜歡破壞法律。

就像在海邊嬉戲的孩子，全心致志地建造沙塔，

再笑著將它們一把打壞。

可是你們在建造沙塔的期間，海洋又把更多的沙帶到岸邊。

當你們毀掉沙塔的時候，海洋也跟著你們同聲歡笑。

的確，海洋永遠陪著天真無邪的人歡笑。

但不把海洋當成生命、不把人為法律當成沙塔的，那些人又如何呢？

他們把生命當作岩石，把法律當成可以在石上刻出自己形象的鑿刀。

厭惡舞者的殘疾者又如何？自己喜愛重軛，卻將森林的麋與鹿視為迷途漂泊者的公牛，又如何呢？

無法蛻去舊皮，卻責罵其他蛇隻無恥裸露的老蛇，又如何呢？

自己早早來到婚宴，酒足飯飽之後疲憊不堪，離去時卻宣稱所有的盛宴一概違規，所有的赴宴者全都犯了法，這人又如何？

對於這些人我還能說些什麼？

只能說他們站在陽光下，卻背對著太陽。

他們只看得到自己的影子，而他們的影子就是他們的法律。

對他們來說，太陽除了會灑下影子之外，又算什麼東西？

而承認法律，不正是彎身在大地上追隨自己的投影嗎？

但是，你這個面對太陽行進的人，

投在大地上的影子哪能妨礙得了你？

御風而行的人，什麼樣的風向標能夠指引你的去路？

如果你砸開自己的枷鎖，卻不撞破他人的牢門，

人為的法律怎麼約束得了你？

如果你盡情舞蹈，卻不踩絆他人的鎖鍊，你何需害怕什麼法律？

如果你扯下衣衫，卻不棄置於他人的路途上，

誰又能將你送庭受審？

奧菲里斯的人們，你們可以悶住鼓聲、鬆開琴弦，

但有誰能命令雲雀噤聲？

# 自由

FREEDOM

有位演說家說，跟我們談談自由。

他回答道：

在城門處，在火爐邊，我曾經看過你們五體投地、膜拜自由。

雖然暴君屠殺奴隸，但奴隸依然在他面前歌功頌德、卑躬屈膝。

是的，我在聖殿周圍的樹叢、堡壘的陰影裡看到，

你們當中最自由的人，卻把自由當成枷鎖手銬來披戴。

我的心在胸中淌血；

因為唯有你把追尋自由的慾望視為枷鎖，

只有你不再把自由當成目標與成就的時候，

你才能獲得自由。

然後享有真正的自由。

你才能赤裸裸又毫無拘束地超越它們，

而是讓這些事情束縛你的生命，

真正的自由，並不是白晝無憂無愁、黑夜毫無匱乏哀痛，

但是除非你打破這條鎖鍊，不然你要如何超越日日夜夜。

你在理解的黎明時分，用鎖鍊綑綁了你的正午時刻，

事實上，你稱之為自由的東西，是這些鎖鍊裡最為堅實的，

雖說鍊環在陽光中晶晶發亮而弄花你的雙眼。

你為了尋求自由而拋下的，不正是自我的碎片？

如果你想廢除的是不公正的法律，那法律也是你當初親手寫在自己額頭上的。

焚燬法律典籍，或是將海水傾倒於法官的額頭上，也無法抹消不公正的法律。

如果你想罷黜獨裁者，先確定你已經摧毀他在你內心樹立的寶座。

暴君如何能夠統治自由與尊嚴的人？

除非自由裡已有專制，尊嚴裡已有恥辱？

如果你想拋開的是憂慮，

那麼憂慮其實是你自找的，而非他人強加給你的。

如果你想驅散的是恐懼，

那麼恐懼其實源自你的內心，而不在你懼怕的對象手裡。

的確，渴望的與恐懼的、厭惡的與珍惜的、追尋的與逃避的，

這一切事物時時相偎相依，都在你的存在之內運行。

這些事物在你之中活動遊移，如同相依相隨的光與影。

當陰影逐漸隱逝不在，流連不去的光就成了另一道光的陰影。

同理，當你的自由擺脫桎梏時，就會成為更大自由的桎梏。

# 理性與熱情

REASON
AND
PASSION

女祭司再次開口並說，請跟我們談談理性與熱情。

他回答：

你的靈魂常常像個戰場，理性判斷在那裡與熱情渴望交戰不休。

但願我是你靈魂裡的和平使者，就能把你本質裡的衝突對立化為一致和諧。

可是除非你自己也是和平使者，不，除非你深愛自己的一切本質，否則我又如何辦得到？

你的理性與熱情是靈魂航行的船舵與風帆。

如果你的風帆或船舵故障了，

你就只能隨波顛簸漂流，或是滯留在汪洋之中。

如果單由理性支配，理性會變成侷限的力量。

而熱情若不加約束，會成為將自己焚毀的烈焰。

因此，讓你的靈魂將理性提升到熱情所在的高度，

使它得以展喉高歌；

讓你的靈魂以理性指引熱情的方向，

使你的熱情得以日日重生，宛如從灰燼中振翅飛騰的鳳凰。

我希望你將判斷與慾望奉為自己家裡的貴賓。

你當然不會禮遇一位而冷落另一位；

因為厚此薄彼就會同時失去雙方的愛戴與忠誠。

你端坐於群山圍繞的白楊涼蔭裡，

品嚐遠方田野與草地的平靜安寧——

願你的心默唸：「上帝在理性中休憩。」

暴風雨來襲，勁風搖撼森林，雷電宣告穹蒼的威嚴——

願你的心敬畏地說：「上帝在熱情中行動。」

既然你是上帝領域裡的一絲氣息、上帝森林裡的一枚樹葉，

你也應該在理性中休憩，在熱情中行動。

# 痛苦

PAIN

有個女人開口：「跟我們談談痛苦。」

他說：

你的痛苦就是原本裹住理解的外殼破裂了。

如同果核必須裂開，讓果仁得到陽光的照拂，你也必須經歷痛苦。

如果你的心能對日常生活的奇蹟時常保持好奇，

痛苦帶來的驚奇並不亞於喜樂；

你要接納內心的季節變換，如同你向來接受田地裡的季節更迭。

你會安詳地觀望自己的哀傷寒冬過去。

你的痛苦大多是自己的選擇。

是你內心的醫生用來療癒你病痛自我的苦藥。

信賴那個醫生，緘默平靜地飲下他那帖藥方吧：

雖說他下手又重又狠，指引他的卻是上帝溫柔的手，

他端來的藥杯，雖然燙灼你的嘴唇，

卻是上帝用祂聖淚滋潤過的泥土所塑造出來的。

# 自知

SELF-
KNOWLEDGE

有個男人說，跟我們談談自知吧。

他回答道：

你的心在靜默之中知曉白晝與黑夜的祕密，

但你的耳朵卻渴望聽見你內在知識的聲音。

你想透過話語來認識思維向來熟知的一切。

你想用手指觸摸夢想的赤裸軀體。

你原本就該這麼做。

你靈魂裡的暗泉必會湧起，淙淙流向大海；

你內心無盡深處的寶藏會展露在你的眼前。

但不要用秤子來衡量你未知的寶藏；

不要用量桿或錘繩來度量你知識的深度。

因為自我是無邊無際、無從估量的大海。

不要說「我找到真理」，而要說「我找到一則真理。」

不要說「我發現靈魂的道路」，

而要說「我遇見在我道路上漫步的靈魂。」

因為靈魂會在所有的道路上漫步。

靈魂不會依循直線行進，也不像蘆葦那般筆直生長。

靈魂會開展綻放，有如花瓣無數的蓮花。

# 教導

## TEACHING

接著有位老師說，跟我們談談教導。

他說：

別人給你的啟發，無不是早在你知識曙光裡半睡半醒的東西。

跟門徒一同在聖殿陰影裡漫步的老師，傳授給人的不是他的智慧，而是他的信念與愛心。

倘若他真有智慧，就不會令你進入他的智慧屋宇，

而會引導你走向你自己的心靈門口。

天文學家可以跟你談談自己對宇宙的理解，卻無法把他的理解給你。

音樂家可以吟唱天地間的韻律供你聆賞，卻不能給你捕捉那韻律的耳朵，也無法給你呼應那韻律的歌喉。

精通數學的人可以暢談度量衡的領域，卻無法引導你到那裡去。

一人的洞見無法外借羽翼給別人。

在上帝的認知裡，你們是不同的個體，

因此你們也必須單獨認識上帝與各自理解大地。

# 友誼

## FRIENDSHIP

有個青年說，跟我們談談友誼。

他回答道：

你的朋友就是你的需求得到回應。

他就是你用愛播種、用感恩收成的田地。

他是你的餐桌與壁爐。

你會帶著飢餓來找他，到他那裡尋求安寧。

當你朋友傾訴心聲時，你不用害怕在自己的心裡說「不」，想在心裡說「是」也無須壓抑。

當他靜默不語的時候，你的心不會停止傾聽他的心；

在友誼裡，即使默默無語，所有的思緒、慾望與期待也都會在無

聲的喜樂裡，孕生出來並共同分享。

跟朋友分離的時候，你不會悲傷；

因為他不在場的時候，你在他身上最欣賞的特質會變得更加突出，

如同登山者在平原上遠眺，可以將山峰看得格外分明。

除了深化心靈之外，友誼不該有任何企圖。

只圖揭露自身謎團的愛，並不是真愛，

而是投撒出來的一面網子：只會網住無益的東西。

把你最好的，獻給你的朋友。

如果他一定要知道你的低潮，也要讓他曉得你洪水滔滔的時候。

如果你找朋友只是為了打發時間，那算什麼朋友？

要為了體驗生命才去找他。

朋友要填滿的是你的需求，而不是你的空虛。

但願在友誼的甜美裡，充滿歡笑與樂趣的分享。

在微小事物的露珠裡，心會覺得自己的清晨，並得以煥然一新。

# 說話

## TALKING

有個學者說，請談談說話這件事。

他回答道：

當你開口說話，就是不再跟思想和平共處的時候。

當你無法繼續安居於內心的孤寂裡，轉而移居於唇舌之上，聲音就成了娛樂與消遣。

在你大多的談話裡，思想有一半遭到扼殺。

因為思想是空中之鳥，在話語的牢籠之中或能展翅，卻無法自由翱翔。

你們當中有些人因為害怕獨處而追隨饒舌健談的人。

獨處的靜寂會讓這些人看見赤裸的自我，於是一心想要閃躲。

還有些人說話，卻在缺乏知識與遠見的狀況下，揭露了連自己也不懂的真理。

有些人的內心存有真理，卻不訴諸於言語。

在這類人的胸懷中，靈魂在富有韻律的靜默之中棲息。

你在路邊或市集遇見朋友的時候，

讓內心的靈魂帶動你的嘴唇、引導你的舌頭。

讓你聲音中的聲音，對著他的耳中之耳說話；

因為他的靈魂會保存你內心的真理，如同美酒的滋味長駐心間，

雖然酒的色澤已遭遺忘、酒器不復存在。

# 時間

## TIME

有個天文學家說，大師，時間又如何呢？

他答道：

你會量測不可測也無法量的時間。

你根據時序與季節，調整自己的行為，甚至指引自己心靈的航程。

你把時間當成溪流，端坐堤岸，眼望溪水奔流。

但是你內心裡的永恆，會意識到生命的永恆，

知道昨日不過是今天的回憶，明日不過是今天的夢境。

知道在你內心歌唱默想的，依然棲居於最初將星辰撒入太空的太
初時刻之內。

你們當中有誰不覺得，自己的愛擁有無邊的力量？
可是又有誰不覺得，那份愛雖然無窮無盡，
卻含藏於自己存在的核心裡，
不會在種種愛的思緒、種種愛的行為之中流轉遊移？

時間不就跟愛一樣，不可分割又無所謂快慢？
可是如果你在心中非得用季節來測量劃分時間，
就讓每個季節蘊含其他季節吧。
就讓今日用回憶擁抱過去，用渴望擁抱未來。

# 善與惡

GOOD
AND EVIL

城裡有位長者說，跟我們談談善與惡。

他答道：

我可以談談你內在的善，卻無法談你內在的惡。

因為惡不就是受到飢餓乾渴所折磨的善嗎？

的確，當善挨餓的時候，會不惜前往闇暗的洞穴裡覓食；

乾渴的時候，會不惜飲用停滯的死水。

你跟自己和諧一致時，就是善的。

你無法跟自己和諧一致時，你也不見得是惡的。

因為分裂的房子，未必就是一窩盜賊；只是分裂的房子罷了。

沒了舵的船，在險象環生的小島之間漫無目的地漂蕩，

但不至於沉入海底。

你努力奉獻自己，你就是善的。

可是你如果為自己謀利，也不算是惡的。

因為當你謀取己利的時候，你只不過是緊攀著大地、吸吮她胸脯乳汁的根。

果實當然不會對根說，

「效法我吧，成熟飽滿，時時獻出自己的豐饒。」

因為對果實來說，施予是種必要，

正如對根來說，收受是種必要。

你在言談之中保持全然的清醒，你就是善的。

可是你在睡夢中任由舌頭亂動、胡言囈語，你也不是惡的。

即使是結結巴巴的話語，也能強化虛弱的舌頭。

前拐腳跛行。

可是你們當中強壯敏捷的人，不要自以為好意，刻意在殘疾者面

可是你們當中強壯敏捷的人，不要自以為好意，刻意在殘疾者面

即使是跛行的人也不會倒退走。

可是當你瘸瘸拐拐往目標走去時，也不是惡的。

當你踩著無畏的步伐、堅定邁向目標時，你是善的。

你的善表現在無數的事物上；

當你不善的時候，也不是惡的。

你只是懶散怠惰罷了。

可惜公鹿無法把敏捷教給烏龜。

你的善，就在你對大我的渴望裡；

而那種渴望，你們人人的心裡都有。

不過，在你們某些人的內心裡，

那份渴望就像是滔滔急流，

夾帶著山坡的祕密與森林的樂章奔湧入海。

而在其他人的內心，

那種渴望有如平緩的溪流，

在蜿蜒曲折之中迷失了自己，在流往海岸的路途上徘徊流連。

可是擁有諸多渴望的人，不要對清心寡欲的人說，

「你為什麼遲緩蹣跚？」

因為真正善的人不會問赤身裸體的人「你的衣服呢？」

更不會問無家可歸的人「你的家怎麼了？」

# 祈禱

PRAYER

接著有位女祭司說，跟我們談談祈禱。

他答道：

你在愁苦與匱乏的時候祈禱；

願你也在喜樂滿溢、豐足無缺的日子裡祈禱。

禱告不就是將自我擴展到靈動的蒼穹裡嗎？

如果你向太空傾注黑暗，可以得到慰藉；

那麼，傾倒內心的曙光也會獲得喜悅。

當靈魂召喚你去祈禱的時候，你卻只能不住地哭泣；

靈魂將會反覆勵勉哭泣的你，直到你再度展露笑顏。

當你祈禱，你會升騰入空，與當下正在禱告的人相遇。

而這些人，你只能藉由禱告相會。

因此，當你造訪那座無形聖殿時，

只能是為了狂喜與甜美的交流，別無其他目的。

因為如果你進入那座殿堂，只是為了開口索求，那麼你將一無所獲；

如果你進入殿堂是為了貶抑自己，你將無法得到提升；

或者如果你進入殿堂，是為了替他人祈求好處，你將不會得到垂聽。

你單是進入無形的殿堂，就已足夠。

我無法教導你該如何用言語禱告。

上帝不會傾聽你的話語，除非祂親自透過你的唇舌道出那些言語。

我無法教導你海洋的、森林的與山脈的禱詞。

可是，你們這些生於山脈、森林與海洋的人，

卻可以在內心找到它們的禱詞；

如果你在靜寂的黑夜裡凝神諦聽，

就會聽到山脈、森林與海洋默默說著：

「我們的上帝，祢是我們長了翅翼的自我。

祢的意志，在我們內心行使意志。

祢的慾望，在我們內心裡表達慾望。

祢在我們內心的衝動，想把我們的黑夜化為白晝；

而這些黑夜白晝都屬於祢。

我們無法向祢開口索求什麼，

因為祢早在我們內心浮現需求以前，就已經洞悉⋯

祢就是我們的需求，祢把更多的自己賜給我們，

就等於給了我們一切。」

# 享樂

## PLEASURE

接著，每年走訪此城一次的隱士趨前說道，跟我們談談享樂。

他答道：

享樂是首自由之歌，但不是自由。

它是你慾望的綻放，但不是慾望的果實。

它是向高峰呼喚的低谷，但不低也不高。

它是在囚籠裡振翅飛翔的東西，卻不是受到包圍的空間。

是的，享樂確實是首自由之歌。

我希望你們能盡情唱它，但不希望你們因此迷失自己的心。

你們有些青年把享樂當成一切來追求，因而遭到批評譴責。

我不會批評譴責他們，我會任由他們去追求。

因為他們會找到歡樂，但找到的卻不僅僅是歡樂；

享樂有七個姊妹，連她們當中最差的，都要比享樂更美。

你們難道不曾聽過，有人挖土掘根卻尋得了寶藏？

你們有些長者抱著懊悔去回憶享樂，

彷彿享樂是酒酣耳熱時犯下的過錯。

可是，懊悔是心裡的陰霾，而不是懲罰。

他應該帶著感恩回憶享樂，如同憶起夏日的收成。

但是，如果懊悔能為他們帶來慰藉，就讓他們得到慰藉吧。

你們當中有些人不如追求享樂者年輕，也還沒有回憶享樂者年老；

這些人害怕追求與回憶，於是閃避一切的享樂，

生怕冷落心靈或觸怒心靈。

因此，雖然他們用顫抖的雙手掘土尋根，卻也會找到寶藏。

但是連他們的捨棄當中，都含有享樂的成分。

可是告訴我，誰會觸怒心靈呢？

夜鶯會冒犯寂靜的黑夜嗎？螢火蟲會惹惱星辰嗎？

你們的火焰或煙霧會成為風的負擔嗎？

你難道認為，心靈是你可以用木棍攪濁的一潭止水嗎？

你拒絕讓自己享樂，常常只是把慾望積藏於你存在的深處而已。

誰曉得今天暫時擱置不理的東西，會不會等著在明天浮現？

連你的身體都懂得天生權利與合理需求，不肯受到矇騙。

你的身體就是你靈魂的豎琴，要用它奏出美妙的音樂或是嘈雜的噪音，完全取決於你自己。

現在你在內心裡問：「我們要怎麼區分享樂裡的好與壞呢？」

到你的田地與花園去，你就會明白，

採集花蜜是蜜蜂的享樂，可是把蜜獻給蜂，也是花的享樂。

因為對蜜蜂來說，花朵是生命的泉源；

對花朵來說，蜜蜂是愛的信使，

對蜂蜜跟花朵來說，施予享樂與接受享樂，既是需求也是狂喜。

奧菲里斯的人們，仿效花朵跟蜜蜂享受歡樂吧。

# 美

BEAUTY

有個詩人說，跟我們談談美。

他回答道：

除非美本身就是你的道路與你的嚮導，否則你要到哪裡尋覓美，又該如何找到她？

除非她是你話語的織工，否則你要怎麼談論她？

冤屈受創的人說，「美是仁慈與溫柔。如同年輕母親在我們當中漫步，對自己的榮耀半帶羞澀。」

熱情奔放的人說，「不，美是強大可畏的東西。

有如暴風雨，搖撼我們腳下的大地、震撼我們頂上的天際。」

疲乏睏倦的人說：「美是輕柔的呢喃。她在我們的心靈裡訴說。

她的聲音屈服於我們的靜默，好似薄弱的光線因為害怕陰影而顫

抖。」

可是，躁動不安的人說，「我們聽到她在群山之間吶喊，

奔蹄、振翅與獅吼伴隨著她的呼喊一同傳來。」

夜裡，城裡的守夜人說，「美會隨著曙光從東方升起。」

正午，勞動者與旅人說，「我們看過她從夕陽的窗口，探出身子俯

瞰大地。」

寒冬，受雪所困的人說，「她伴隨著春季降臨，一同躍上山丘。」

盛夏，收割者在暑氣裡說，「我們看到她伴著秋葉起舞，髮梢沾著

點點雪花。」

——這些就是你們對美的看法。

可是，老實說你們講的不是美，

而是尚未滿足的需求，美不是需求而是狂喜。

它既不是乾渴的嘴，也不是往前探出的空手，

而是熾熱的心與迷醉的靈魂。

不是你們會看到的影像，也不是你們會聽聞的歌曲，

而是縱使合上眼睛也見得著的影像，掩上耳朵也聽得見的歌曲

不是粗皺樹皮裡的汁液，更不是連接指爪的翅翼，

而是永遠繁花盛放的一座花園，永遠展翅飛翔的一群天使。

奧菲里斯的人們，

美就是生命揭去面紗、露出神聖容顏。

但你就是生命，你就是那面紗。

美就是在鏡中凝望自己的永恆。

但你們就是永恆，你們就是那面鏡。

# 宗教

RELIGION

有位老祭司說，跟我們談談宗教。

他說：

我今天談的不都是這個嗎？

所有的作為跟省思不都是宗教？

雙手忙著砍劈石頭或操作織布機時，在靈魂裡躍動的讚嘆與驚喜，

雖然既非作為，也非省思，但不也都是宗教嗎？

誰能把自己的信仰跟行動，或是信念跟職業區分開來呢？

誰能把時間攤在面前並說，「這段給神，這段給我自己；

這截給我的靈魂，另一截給我的軀體？」

你所有的時光都會振翅穿越空間，從自我飛往自我。

把道德當成錦衣華服穿戴上身的人，還不如一絲不掛；

風兒跟太陽不會在他的肌膚上扯出坑洞來。

用倫理來界定自己行為的人，等於將自己的鳴鳥囚禁在籠子裡。

最自由的歌曲不會透過欄杆跟鐵絲傳來。

有人把敬拜當成是扇可開也可關的窗戶，這樣的人一定尚未探訪

過自己靈魂的屋宇——那兒的窗戶永遠從黎明開到黎明。

你的日常生活就是你的聖殿跟你的宗教。

不管你何時進去，隨身帶著你的一切吧。

把犁具、燬爐、木槌跟魯特琴都帶去，

這些都是你出於需要或樂趣所製造的物品。

因為冥想之時，你無法超越成就的高度，

也無法跌落得比失敗更低。

帶著所有的人同去：

因為敬拜之際，你無法飛得比他們的希望更高，

也無法把自我貶抑得比他們的絕望更低。

如果你想要認識上帝，別一心想要破解謎題。

環顧四周，你會看到祂正跟你的孩子嬉戲。

仰望天空，你會看到祂正在雲端漫步，

從閃電裡伸出臂膀，在雨中翩然降臨。

你會看到祂在花叢裡微笑，在樹林間飛身揮手。

# 死亡

DEATH

接著艾蜜特拉開口了，她說，我們現在想請教死亡的事。

他回答道：

你們想知道死亡的祕密。

可是除非你們往生命的核心裡尋找，否則如何找得到？

貓頭鷹的夜光眼看不清白晝，無法揭開光的奧秘。

如果你真的想一睹死亡的心靈，就向生命的軀體大大敞開你的心。

因為生死一體，如同河海同源。

你們盼望與慾望的深處，默默藏著你們關於來生的知識；

如同種子在冰雪下作夢，你的心也夢想著春天。

要信任夢境，因為裡面潛藏通往永恆的大門。

你們對死亡的恐懼，只不過是牧羊人站在國王面前時的顫抖，

而國王即將伸手賜他榮耀。牧羊人的身上將會留下國王的印記。

牧羊人在顫抖之餘，難道不會覺得歡喜？

然而更讓他耿耿於懷的，不正是自己的顫抖嗎？

什麼是死亡？不就是在風中赤裸佇立、消融於陽光裡？

什麼是停止呼吸？不過是將氣息從騷動不止的潮汐解脫出來，

好讓它升騰擴張、毫無窒礙地追尋上帝？

唯有啜飲靜默之河，你才可能真正歌唱。

唯有抵達山巔，你才可能開始攀登向上。

唯有當大地佔有你的四肢，你才可能真正手舞足蹈。

# 告別

## THE FAREWELL

日暮時分。

預言家艾蜜特拉說，願神祝福今日、此地，以及你這開口訴說的心靈。

他回答，難道我只是個訴說的人嗎？

我不也是傾聽的人嗎？

然後他步下聖殿的階梯，眾人全都尾隨在後。

他登船站上甲板。

他再次面對眾人高聲說道：

奧菲里斯的人們，風吩咐我離開你們。

雖說我沒有風那麼急躁，但我非得離去。

我們漂泊者永遠在尋覓更寂寞的道路，不會在過完一日的地方展

開另一天，也不會在夕陽離開我們的地方迎接日出。

大地沉睡的時候，我們依然跋涉不停。

我們是頑強的植物種子，到了核心飽滿的成熟時刻，

就會被交託給風，然後四散紛飛。

我在你們當中度過的時日不長，而我所說的話語更為簡短。

可是，萬一我的聲音在你們的耳裡淡去，我的愛在你們的記憶中

消隱，我就會再回來。

我會以更豐富的心、更順服心靈的唇舌說話。

是的，我會隨著潮浪歸來，

雖然死亡可能掩蔽我，更深的沉默可能包圍我，

但我會再次尋求你們的理解。

而且我的尋求將不會白白落空。

要是我說的話含有真理，那真理將會以更清晰的聲音，

以更親近你們思想的話語，來揭露自己。

奧菲里斯的人們，

我將隨風而去，但不會墜入虛空；

倘若今日尚未滿足你們的需求、尚未實現我的愛，

那麼就讓我們許下來日再續的承諾。

人的需求會改變，但他的愛不會改變，

他對愛應該滿足需求的這種渴望也不會改變。

因此，你們要明白，我將會從更深的靜寂歸來。

黎明時分消散的霧氣，雖然只會在田野上留下露珠，
但會升空聚積成雲，繼而化為雨滴降臨。
我與霧氣沒有不同。

寂靜的黑夜裡，
我在你們的街道上漫步，我的心靈進入你們的屋宇，
我的心裡有你們的心跳聲，你們的吐息拂過我的臉。
我認識你們所有人。

是的，我熟知你們的喜樂與痛楚；
你們入睡的時候，你們的夢境就是我的夢。
常常身處你們之中的我，有如群山圍繞的湖泊。
我映照出你們心中的山峰與蜿蜒斜坡，
甚至映照出如羊群般掠過你們心頭的思緒與渴望。

你們孩童的笑聲有如溪流，青年的渴望宛如河川，朝著我寂靜的湖泊流淌而來。

溪流與河川抵達我的湖心時，依然歌唱不歇。

可是比笑聲更甜美、比渴望更深遠的東西，也一同來到了我這邊：

那就是你們內在的廣闊無垠；

你們在那巨人之內只不過是細胞與筋腱。

在他的吟頌裡，你們的歌唱只不過是無聲的悸動。

在這巨人之內，你們也遼闊無邊；

唯有注視著他，我才會看見你們並且深愛你們。

因為愛所能跨越的距離，不都在那片遼闊的領地之內嗎？

什麼樣的洞見、期盼與臆測，足以飛越那片領空？

你們內在的巨人，有如覆滿蘋果花的巨大櫟樹。

他的力量將你們與大地連結相繫，他的芬芳使你們升入空中，

他的恆久讓你們不朽。

有人告訴你們：如同鍊子，你們跟最脆弱的鍊環一般虛弱。

這話只說對了一半。

你們也跟最強韌的鍊環一般堅強。

用你們最微小的行為來衡量你，等於是憑著薄弱的浪花碎沫，來計

算大海的威力。

用你們的失敗來批判你們，等於是責怪季節的變換不定。

是的，你們就像大海，

雖然重重擱淺的船隻在你們的海岸上等待漲潮，

但是，如同海洋，你們也無法催起海潮來到。

你們也像四季，

雖然在冬天，你們否認自己的春天，

但是，在你們內心歇息的春天，依然睡眼惺忪地微笑，

並不會受到冒犯。

我只是把你們思維裡早已明瞭的，化為言語說出來給你們聽。

「他對我們讚許有加。他只看到我們內在的美好。」

不要以為我說這些事情，是為了讓你們對彼此說：

口語相傳的知識，不就是無言知識的影子嗎？

你們的思維跟我的話語，就是從封存記憶裡湧來的海濤，

而那份回憶記錄著我們的昨日往昔，記錄著古遠的歲月——

當時大地還不認識我們也不認識自己。

記錄著黑夜，當時大地渾沌混亂。

智者來到你們身邊，傳授智慧給你們。

我來則是為了求取你們的智慧：

看哪！我找到了比智慧更偉大的東西，

就是在你們內心越燒越旺的心靈烈焰。

你們卻不理會它的擴張，反倒只顧哀嘆時光的凋零。

唯有一心追尋肉身生命的生命，才會懼怕墳塋。

這裡沒有墳塋。

這些山脈與平原是搖籃，也是墊腳石。

不管你們何時路過安葬祖先的田野時，

細看一眼，就會看見自己跟孩子手牽手跳舞

的確，你們常常會不自覺地尋求歡樂。

其他人來找你們，憑藉你們的信任而許下黃金般的承諾，而你們將財富、權勢與榮耀賜予了他們。

我給你們的還不及一個承諾，但你們對我卻更加慷慨大量。

你們讓我對生命懷有更深的渴望。

確實，獻給一個人的最大恩賜，莫過於將他的一切目標化為乾渴的嘴唇、將所有生命化作甘泉。

我的榮耀跟回報都在這當中——

不管我何時來這甘泉掬飲，都會發現那股活水本身也是乾渴的；

我喝它的時候，它也在飲我。

因為我不收受禮物，所以你們有些人認為我自恃甚高、過度羞澀。

我的確因為自尊過高而不願收受酬勞，但並不拒絕恩賜。

雖然你們邀我至家中用膳時，我卻到山間摘食莓果，

當你們願意提供住宿時，我卻睡臥於聖殿的門廊下，

不過，不就是因為你們關懷著我的日夜，

才使得我口中的食物嚐來甘美，有美夢環繞我的睡眠？

為此我要特別祝福你們：

以美名自誇的善行會成為詛咒的源頭。

的確，攬鏡自照的善心會化為石頭，

你們付出許多，卻完全不自知。

你們有些人說我孤高冷漠，沉醉在自己的孤寂裡，

你們說，「他只跟森林的樹木互動交流，卻不跟人往來切磋。

他獨坐丘頂，睥睨我們的城市。」

的確，我攀登山丘、在僻地漫遊。

要不是從高處或遠處，我要如何看清你們？

要是不到遠處，如何真正靠近？

你們當中的其他人透過意念默默呼喚我，他們說：

「異鄉人啊異鄉人，喜愛高不可及之處的人，

你為何棲居於老鷹築巢的山巔？

你為何追尋無法企及的東西？

你想用網子捕住什麼狂風暴雨？

你想在空中狩獵什麼虛幻奇禽？

過來加入我們的行列。

下來吧，靠我們的麵包止飢、以我們的美酒解渴。」

他們在自己靈魂的孤獨裡，說了這些事情；

可是如果他們的孤獨更加深刻，

他們就會知道我所尋求的，不過是你們喜樂與痛苦的祕密；

我狩獵的，也只是你們在空中漫步的更大自我。

但獵者也是獵物；

因為從我這把弓射出的箭矢，有不少只為尋覓我的胸膛。

飛翔者也是爬行者；

因為當我在陽光下展開翅膀，落在地上的翅影卻有如烏龜。

身為信仰者的我，也是懷疑者；

我常把手指探進傷口，才能更信任你們、更認識你們。

憑著這份信任與認知，我要說，

你們不受軀殼的束縛，也不受屋宇或田野的侷限。

你的真我，棲居於山巒之上，隨風浪遊四方。

它不會為了取暖而爬向陽光，也不會為了安全而往暗處鑽洞，

而是自由自在的，是籠罩大地、在蒼穹裡遊走的魂靈。

如果這些話語含糊不明，也不要想去釐清。

模糊與朦朧，是萬物的開端而不是盡頭。

我希望你們在記憶裡把我看成開端。

生命與所有的生物，都是在迷霧裡而非水晶裡孕生的。

誰曉得水晶會不會就是衰敗的迷霧？

我希望當你們憶起我的時候，能記得這點：

你們內心看來最屢弱最惶惑的，其實是最剛強也最堅毅的。

支撐強化你們骨骼架構的，不正是你們的氣息嗎？

構築你們的城市並塑造其中萬物的，不正是你們不復記憶的夢想嗎？

如果你們聽得見夢想的呢喃低語，就對其他聲響聽而不聞。

如果你看得見那氣息的潮汐漲落，就對其他一切視而不見，

可是你們看不到也聽不見，那樣倒好。

編織面紗的雙手，會撩起蒙住你雙眼的面紗，

揉捏泥團的手指，會戳穿填塞你耳朵的泥團。

然後你就會看得到，

然後你就會聽得見。

不過你不該哀嘆自己曾經目盲，不該懊悔自己曾經耳聾，

因為到了那天，你將會知曉隱藏於萬事萬物裡的目的，

到時你將會頌揚黑暗，一如你頌贊光明。

語畢，他環顧四周，看到舵手站在舵輪那裡，

時而凝望飽漲的風帆，時而眺望遠方。

他說：

我的船長很有耐心，太有耐心了。

風已吹起，船帆蠢蠢不安；連船舵都乞求指引；

但我的船長依然靜待我沉默下來。

我的船員們聽到了汪洋大海的合唱，卻也耐性十足聽我說話。

現在他們不用再等了——我已準備就緒。

溪流已經奔抵大海，偉大的母親再次將兒子擁入胸懷。

再見了，奧菲里斯的人們。

今日已近尾聲。

它對著我們閉合，如同睡蓮對著明日合攏花瓣。

我們要好好保存在這裡領受的贈予。

如有不足，我們會再相聚，一同向餽贈者伸出雙手。

不要忘記，我到時會回來找你們。

再一會兒，我的渴望將為另一副軀體聚集沙塵與水沫。

再一會兒，在風中小憩片刻之後，會有另一個女人生下我。

眾人再見了。

我曾經與你們共度的青春歲月，再見了。

我們在夢中相逢不過是昨天的事，

你們在我的孤寂中對我歌唱，

而我用你們的渴望在空中築起一座高塔。

但是現在我們的睡眠已經逃離，

夢已盡，不再是黎明。

午時將臨，我們的半寐半明即將全然甦醒。

我們必得分離。

如果我們在記憶的薄暮中相會，

我們將會聚首長談，

而你們會再為我唱起更深沉的歌曲。

如果我們的雙手在另一場夢裡交握，

我們會在空中共築另一座高塔。

他說著便向船員打打手勢，

他們立即起錨解纜、離開停泊地，往東方駛去。

眾人齊心發出一聲吶喊。

聲音有如嘹亮的號角，升入暮色，往外傳向大海。

只有艾蜜特拉默默無語，凝望船隻，直到它消失在霧氣裡。

等人群盡皆散去，她依然獨自佇立在海堤那裡，

在心裡默想他的話語：

「再一會兒，在風中小憩片刻之後，會有另一個女人生下我。」

# 【名家及媒體盛譽】

我喜愛紀伯侖的作品，特別欣賞他的人生哲學以及對愛的追求。他說「愛不佔有，也不被佔有」、「真正偉大的人是不壓制別人，也不受壓制的人。」這些深刻的至理名言在他的作品中比比皆是，深深地感染了幾個世代的讀者。

——中國作家冰心

《先知》具有東方蘇菲精神，書中闡述許多高尚而富有哲理的教誨，加上文筆輕柔優美，有如潺潺流水，散發出迷人的音樂感。

——黎巴嫩文學史家漢納·法胡里

紀伯侖的作品是充滿思想和哲理的深邃海洋。他就像先知，為人類尋求禁錮心靈的解脫之道；他就像導師，在人類心靈播種愛情，在群眾之間傳遞幸福。

——黎巴嫩前駐中國大使法里德·薩瑪赫

《先知》充滿用敘利亞式的美、音樂和理想主義表現出來的真理。它以二十八篇詩文形成了一本小聖經，讓那些對於接受真理有所準備的人們，去閱讀和愛慕。

——《芝加哥晚報》

這是改變我一生的書，裡面的篇章觸及生活的每個層面，為人生諸多疑惑和困境提出簡單明確的解答。當我離家時，我的父母親塞給我一本《先知》，往後它就像是我們家的聖經一般。

——英國知名媒體人Julia Bradbury

《先知》一書談論每個人日常生活中最根本的事物，包括愛、飲食、工作、歡喜與悲傷、兒童、衣物、居住、買賣、罪與罰、自由、享樂、美、宗教及死亡。這些對根本事物深思熟慮之後獲致的結論，紀伯侖將智慧之語說得古老而雋永。然而除此之外，紀伯侖的話語也彰顯出獨特的個人印記。他並未揭示通往幸福的捷徑，也從未提供可掌握的成功之道——他要你深刻地探索自己的內心。

——《紐約時報》

※編後語：紀伯侖的作品蘊含了豐富的社會性和東方精神，是二十世紀阿拉伯新文學道路的開拓者，《先知》為其步入世界文壇的頂峰之作，至今被譯為五十多國語言，流傳全世界。

一九三一年四月十日，紀伯侖病逝於紐約，歸葬黎巴嫩。他的棺木上覆蓋著黎巴嫩和美國國旗，遺體受到成千上萬不分宗教、年齡和國籍的民眾瞻仰與哀悼。在紀伯侖誕辰的一百週年，黎巴嫩政府定名為「紀伯侖年」；同年，聯合國教科文組織將他列為具有世界意義的「世界文化名人」，以茲紀念。

# THE PROPHET
## KAHLIL GIBRAN

國家圖書館出版品預行編目

先知 / 紀伯侖 (Kahlil Gibran) 著；謝靜雯譯. --
初版. -- 新北市：木馬文化出版：遠足文化
發行, 2014.07
　　面；13x19 公分
譯自：The prophet
ISBN 978-986-359-027-9( 平裝 )

865.751　　　　　　　　　　　103011048

# 先知
The Prophet

作　　　者：紀伯侖（Kahlil Gibran）
譯　　　者：謝靜雯
副 社 長：陳瀅如
責任編輯：李嘉琪
美術設計：蔡南昇
內頁編排：優克居有限公司
出　　　版：木馬文化事業股份有限公司
發　　　行：遠足文化事業股份有限公司(讀書共和國出版集團)
地　　　址：231新北市新店區民權路108-2號9樓
電　　　話：(02)2218-1417
傳　　　真：(02)2218-0727
E-mail：service@bookrep.com.tw
郵撥帳號：19588272木馬文化事業股份有限公司
客服專線：0800221029
法律顧問：華洋法律事務所　蘇文生律師
印　　　刷：成陽印刷股份有限公司
初　　　版：2014年7月
初版 8 刷：2024年5月
定　　　價：280元
ISBN：978-986-359-027-9
木馬部落格：http://blog.roodo.com/ecus2005
木馬臉書粉絲團：http://www.facebook.com/ecusbook

# THE PROPHET
## CONTENTS

# THE PROPHET
## CONTENTS

# THE COMING OF THE SHIP

ALMUSTAFA, the chosen and the beloved, who was a dawn unto his own day, had waited twelve years in the city of Orphalese for his ship that was to return and bear him back to the isle of his birth.

And in the twelfth year, on the seventh day of Ielool, the month of reaping, he climbed the hill without the city walls and looked seaward; and he beheld his ship coming with the mist. Then the gates of his heart were flung open, and his joy flew far over the sea.

And he closed his eyes and prayed in the silences of his soul.

❧ ❧ ❧

But as he descended the hill, a sadness came upon him, and he thought in his heart: How shall I go in peace and without sorrow? Nay, not without a wound in the spirit shall I leave this city. Long were the days of pain I have spent within its walls, and long were the nights of aloneness; and who can depart from his pain and his aloneness without regret?

❧ ❧ ❧

Too many fragments of the spirit have I scattered in these streets, and too many are the children of my longing that walk naked among these hills, and I cannot withdraw from them without a burden and an ache. It is not a garment I cast off this day, but a skin that I tear with my own hands. Nor is it a thought I leave behind me, but a heart made sweet with hunger and with thirst.

❧ ❧ ❧

Yet I cannot tarry longer. The sea that calls all things unto her calls me, and I must embark. For to stay, though the hours burn in the night, is to freeze and crystallize and be bound in a mould.

Fain would I take with me all that is here. But how shall I? A voice cannot carry the tongue and the lips that gave it wings. Alone must it seek the ether. And alone and without his nest shall the eagle fly across the sun.

കൗ കൗ കൗ

Now when he reached the foot of the hill, he turned again towards the sea, and he saw his ship approaching the harbour, and upon her prow the mariners, the men of his own land.

കൗ കൗ കൗ

And his soul cried out to them, and he said: Sons of my ancient mother, you riders of the tides, How often have you sailed in my dreams. And now you come in my awakening, which is my deeper dream. Ready am I to go, and my eagerness with sails full set awaits the wind. Only another breath will I breathe in this still air, only another loving look cast backward, And then I shall stand among you, a seafarer among seafarers. And you, vast sea, sleeping mother, Who alone are peace and freedom to the river and the stream, Only another winding will this stream make, only another murmur in this glade, And then I shall come to you, a boundless drop to a boundless ocean.

And as he walked he saw from afar men and women leaving their fields and their vineyards and hastening towards the city gates. And he heard their voices calling his name, and shouting from field to field telling one another of the coming of his ship.

And he said to himself: Shall the day of parting be the day of gathering? And shall it be said that my eve was in truth my dawn? And what shall I give unto him who has left his plough in midfurrow, or to him who has stopped the wheel of his winepress? Shall my heart become a tree heavy-laden with fruit that I may gather and give unto them? And shall my desires flow like a fountain that I may fill their cups? Am I a harp that the hand of the mighty may touch me, or a flute that his breath may pass through me? A seeker of silences am I, and what treasure have I found in silences that I may dispense with confidence? If this is my day of harvest, in what fields have I sowed the seed, and in what unremembered seasons? If this indeed be the hour in which I lift up my lantern, it is not my flame that shall burn therein. Empty and dark shall I raise my lantern, And the guardian of the night shall fill

it with oil and he shall light it also.

⟜⟜⟜

These things he said in words. But much in his heart remained unsaid. For he himself could not speak his deeper secret.

And when he entered into the city all the people came to meet him, and they were crying out to him as with one voice. And the elders of the city stood forth and said: Go not yet away from us. A noontide have you been in our twilight, and your youth has given us dreams to dream.

⟜⟜⟜

No stranger are you among us, nor a guest, but our son and our dearly beloved. Suffer not yet our eyes to hunger for your face.

And the priests and the priestesses said unto him: Let not the waves of the sea separate us now, and the years you have spent in our midst become a memory. You have walked among us a spirit, and your shadow has been a light upon our faces. Much have we loved you. But speechless was our love, and with veils has it been veiled. Yet now it cries aloud unto you, and would stand revealed

before you. And ever has it been that love knows not its own depth until the hour of separation.

ന ന ന

And others came also and entreated him. But he answered them not. He only bent his head; and those who stood near saw his tears falling upon his breast.

ന ന ന

And he and the people proceeded towards the great square before the temple. And there came out of the sanctuary a woman whose name was Almitra. And she was a seeress. And he looked upon her with exceeding tenderness, for it was she who had first sought and believed in him when he had been but a day in their city. And she hailed him, saying: Prophet of God, in quest of the uttermost, long have you searched the distances for your ship. And now your ship has come, and you must needs go. Deep is your longing for the land of your memories and the dwelling-place of your greater desires; and our love would not bind you nor our needs hold you.

ന ന ന

Yet this we ask ere you leave us, that you speak to us and give us

of your truth. And we will give it unto our children, and they unto their children, and it shall not perish. In your aloneness you have watched with our days, and in your wakefulness you have listened to the weeping and the laughter of our sleep. Now therefore disclose us to ourselves, and tell us all that has been shown you of that which is between birth and death.

And he answered: People of Orphalese, of what can I speak save of that which is even now moving within your souls?

# LOVE

‹‹‹◦×◦›››

THEN said Almitra, "Speak to us of Love."

∽ ∽ ∽

And he raised his head and looked upon the people, and there fell a stillness upon them. And with a great voice he said: When love beckons to you, follow him, Though his ways are hard and steep. And when his wings enfold you yield to him, Though the sword hidden among his pinions may wound you. And when he speaks to you believe in him, Though his voice may shatter your dreams as the north wind lays waste the garden.

For even as love crowns you so shall he crucify you. Even as he is for your growth so is he for your pruning. Even as he ascends to your height and caresses your tenderest branches that quiver in the sun, So shall he descend to your roots and shake them in their clinging to the earth. Like sheaves of corn he gathers you unto himself. He threshes you to make you naked. He sifts you to free you from your husks. He grinds you to whiteness. He kneads you until you are pliant; And then he assigns you to his sacred fire, that you may become sacred bread for God's sacred feast.

All these things shall love do unto you that you may know the secrets of your heart, and in that knowledge become a fragment of Life's heart.

But if in your fear you would seek only love's peace and love's pleasure, Then it is better for you that you cover your nakedness and pass out of love's threshing-floor, Into the seasonless world where you shall laugh, but not all of your laughter, and weep, but not all of your tears.

Love gives naught but itself and takes naught but from itself. Love possesses not nor would it be possessed; For love is sufficient unto love.

When you love you should not say, "God is in my heart," but rather, "I am in the heart of God." And think not you can direct the course of love, for love, if it finds you worthy, directs your course.

Love has no other desire but to fulfill itself. But if you love and must needs have desires, let these be your desires: To melt and be like a running brook that sings its melody to the night. To know the pain of too much tenderness. To be wounded by your own understanding of love; And to bleed willingly and joyfully. To wake at dawn with a winged heart and give thanks for another day of loving; To rest at the noon hour and meditate love's ecstasy; To return home at eventide with gratitude; And then to sleep with a prayer for the beloved in your heart and a song of praise upon your lips.

# MARRIAGE

THEN Almitra spoke again and said, "And what of Marriage, master?"

⚬⚬ ⚬⚬ ⚬⚬

And he answered saying: You were born together, and together you shall be for evermore. You shall be together when the white wings of death scatter your days. Aye, you shall be together even in the silent memory of God. But let there be spaces in your togetherness. And let the winds of the heavens dance between you.

Love one another, but make not a bond of love: let it rather be a moving sea between the shores of your souls. Fill each other's cup but drink not from one cup. Give one another of your bread but eat not from the same loaf. Sing and dance together and be joyous, but let each one of you be alone, even as the strings of a lute are alone though they quiver with the same music.

Give your hearts, but not into each other's keeping. For only the hand of Life can contain your hearts. And stand together yet not too near together: For the pillars of the temple stand apart, And the oak tree and the cypress grow not in each other's shadow.

# CHILDREN

$A$ND a woman who held a babe against her bosom said, "Speak to us of Children."

ⅽↄↄ ⅽↄↄ ⅽↄↄ

And he said: Your children are not your children. They are the sons and daughters of Life's longing for itself. They come through you but not from you, And though they are with you yet they belong not to you.

ⅽↄↄ ⅽↄↄ ⅽↄↄ

You may give them your love but not your thoughts, For they have their own thoughts. You may house their bodies but not their souls, For their souls dwell in the house of tomorrow, which you cannot visit, not even in your dreams. You may strive to be like them, but seek not to make them like you. For life goes not backward nor tarries with yesterday. You are the bows from which your children as living arrows are sent forth.

The archer sees the mark upon the path of the infinite, and He bends you with His might that His arrows may go swift and far. Let your bending in the Archer's hand be for gladness; For even as He loves the arrow that flies, so He loves also the bow that is stable.

# GIVING

━━━━◦◇◦━━━━

THEN said a rich man, "Speak to us of Giving."

∽∽∽

And he answered: You give but little when you give of your possessions. It is when you give of yourself that you truly give. For what are your possessions but things you keep and guard for fear you may need them tomorrow? And tomorrow, what shall tomorrow bring to the over-prudent dog burying bones in the track less sand as he follows the pilgrims to the holy city? And what is fear of need but need itself? Is not dread of thirst when your well is

full, the thirst that is unquenchable? There are those who give little of the much which they have—and they give it for recognition and their hidden desire makes their gifts unwholesome. And there are those who have little and give it all. These are the believers in life and the bounty of life, and their coffer is never empty.

There are those who give with joy, and that joy is their reward. And there are those who give with pain, and that pain is their baptism. And there are those who give and know not pain in giving, nor do they seek joy, nor give with mindfulness of virtue; They give as in yonder valley the myrtle breathes its fragrance into space. Through the hands of such as these God speaks, and from behind their eyes He smiles Upon the earth.

It is well to give when asked, but it is better to give unasked, through understanding; And to the open-handed the search for one who shall receive is joy greater than giving. And is there aught you would withhold? All you have shall some day be given; Therefore give now, that the season of giving may be yours and not your inheritors'.

You often say, "I would give, but only to the deserving." The trees in your orchard say not so, nor the flocks in your pasture. They give that they may live, for to withhold is to perish. Surely he who is worthy to receive his days and his nights is worthy of all else from you. And he who has deserved to drink from the ocean of life deserves to fill his cup from your little stream. And what desert greater shall there be, than that which lies in the courage and the confidence, nay the charity, of receiving? And who are you that men should rend their bosom and unveil their pride, that you may see their worth naked and their pride unabashed? See first that you yourself deserve to be a giver, and an instrument of giving. For in truth it is life that gives unto life—while you, who deem yourself a giver, are but a witness.

And you receivers—and you are all receivers—assume no weight of gratitude, lest you lay a yoke upon yourself and upon him who gives. Rather rise together with the giver on his gifts as on wings; For to be overmindful of your debt is to doubt his generosity who has the free-hearted earth for mother, and God for father.

# EATING AND DRINKING

THEN an old man, a keeper of an inn, said, "Speak to us of Eating and Drinking."

⟋⟋

And he said: Would that you could live on the fragrance of the earth, and like an air plant be sustained by the light. But since you must kill to eat, and rob the newly born of its mother's milk to quench your thirst, let it then be an act of worship, And let your board stand an altar on which the pure and the innocent of forest and plain are sacrificed for that which is purer and still more

innocent in man.

When you kill a beast say to him in your heart: "By the same power that slays you, I too am slain; and I too shall be consumed. For the law that delivered you into my hand shall deliver me into a mightier hand. Your blood and my blood is naught but the sap that feeds the tree of heaven."

∽ ∽ ∽

And when you crush an apple with your teeth, say to it in your heart: "Your seeds shall live in my body, And the buds of your tomorrow shall blossom in my heart, And your fragrance shall be my breath, And together we shall rejoice through all the seasons."

∽ ∽ ∽

And in the autumn, when you gather the grapes of your vineyards for the winepress, say in your heart: "I too am a vineyard, and my fruit shall be gathered for the winepress, And like new wine I shall be kept in eternal vessels." And in winter, when you draw the wine, let there be in your heart a song for each cup; And let there be in the song a remembrance for the autumn days, and for the vineyard, and for the winepress.

# WORK

THEN a ploughman said, "Speak to us of Work."

And he answered, saying: You work that you may keep pace with the earth and the soul of the earth. For to be idle is to become a stranger unto the seasons, and to step out of life's procession that marches in majesty and proud submission towards the infinite.

When you work you are a flute through whose heart the

whispering of the hours turns to music. Which of you would be a reed, dumb and silent, when all else sings together in unison?

∽ ∽ ∽

Always you have been told that work is a curse and labour a misfortune. But I say to you that when you work you fulfill a part of earth's furthest dream, assigned to you when that dream was born, And in keeping yourself with labour you are in truth loving life, And to love life through labour is to be intimate with life's inmost secret.

∽ ∽ ∽

But if you in your pain call birth an affliction and the support of the flesh a curse written upon your brow, then I answer that naught but the sweat of your brow shall wash away that which is written.

∽ ∽ ∽

You have been told also that life is darkness, and in your weariness you echo what was said by the weary. And I say that life is indeed darkness save when there is urge, And all urge is blind save when there is know ledge. And all knowledge is vain save when there is work, And all work is empty save when there is love;

And when you work with love you bind your self to yourself, and to one another, and to God.

❧ ❧ ❧

And what is it to work with love? It is to weave the cloth with threads drawn from your heart, even as if your beloved were to wear that cloth. It is to build a house with affection, even as if your beloved were to dwell in that house. It is to sow seeds with tenderness and reap the harvest with joy, even as if your beloved were to eat the fruit. It is to charge all things you fashion with a breath of your own spirit, And to know that all the blessed dead are standing about you and watching.

❧ ❧ ❧

Often have I heard you say, as if speaking in sleep, "He who works in marble, and finds the shape of his own soul in the stone, is nobler than he who ploughs the soil. And he who seizes the rainbow to lay it on a cloth in the likeness of man, is more than he who makes the sandals for our feet."

❧ ❧ ❧

But I say, not in sleep, but in the overwakefulness of noontide,

that the wind speaks not more sweetly to the giant oaks than to the least of all the blades of grass; And he alone is great who turns the voice of the wind into a song made sweeter by his own loving.

⁓ ⁓ ⁓

Work is love made visible. And if you cannot work with love but only with distaste, it is better that you should leave your work and sit at the gate of the temple and take alms of those who work with joy. For if you bake bread with indifference, you bake a bitter bread that feeds but half man's hunger. And if you grudge the crushing of the grapes, your grudge distills a poison in the wine.

⁓ ⁓ ⁓

And if you sing though as angels, and love not the singing, you muffle man's ears to the voices of the day and the voices of the night.

# JOY AND SORROW

⟶⟨⟩⟵

THEN a woman said, "Speak to us of Joy and Sorrow."

∽ ∽ ∽

And he answered: Your joy is your sorrow unmasked. And the selfsame well from which your laughter rises was oftentimes filled with your tears. And how else can it be? The deeper that sorrow carves into your being, the more joy you can contain. Is not the cup that holds your wine the very cup that was burned in the potter's oven? And is not the lute that soothes your spirit the very wood that was hollowed with knives?

When you are joyous, look deep into your heart and you shall find it is only that which has given you sorrow that is giving you joy. When you are sorrowful, look again in your heart, and you shall see that in truth you are weeping for that which has been your delight.

⌒⌒⌒

Some of you say, "Joy is greater than sorrow," and others say, "Nay, sorrow is the greater."

But I say unto you, they are inseparable. Together they come, and when one sits alone with you at your board, remember that the other is asleep upon your bed.

⌒⌒⌒

Verily you are suspended like scales between your sorrow and your joy. Only when you are empty are you at standstill and balanced. When the treasure-keeper lifts you to weigh his gold and his silver, needs must your joy or your sorrow rise or fall.

# HOUSES

THEN a mason came forth and said, "Speak to us of Houses."

⁓⁓⁓

And he answered and said: Build of your imaginings a bower in the wilderness ere you build a house within the city walls. For even as you have home-comings in your twilight, so has the wanderer in you, the ever-distant and alone. Your house is your larger body. It grows in the sun and sleeps in the stillness of the night; and it is not dreamless. Does not your house dream? and dreaming, leave the city for grove or hilltop?

Would that I could gather your houses into my hand, and like a sower scatter them in forest and meadow. Would the valleys were your streets, and the green paths your alleys, that you might seek one another through vineyards, and come with the fragrance of the earth in your garments. But these things are not yet to be.

∽∽∽∽∽

In their fear your forefathers gathered you too near together. And that fear shall endure a little longer. A little longer shall your city walls separate your hearths from your fields.

∽∽∽∽∽

And tell me, people of Orphalese, what have you in these houses? And what is it you guard with fastened doors? Have you peace, the quiet urge that reveals your power? Have you remembrances, the glimmering arches that span the summits of the mind? Have you beauty, that leads the heart from things fashioned of wood and stone to the holy mountain? Tell me, have you these in your houses? Or have you only comfort, and the lust for comfort, that stealthy thing that enters the house a guest, and then becomes a host, and then a master?

Ay, and it becomes a tamer, and with hook and scourge makes puppets of your larger desires.

Though its hands are silken, its heart is of iron. It lulls you to sleep only to stand by your bed and jeer at the dignity of the flesh. It makes mock of your sound senses, and lays them in thistledown like fragile vessels. Verily the lust for comfort murders the passion of the soul, and then walks grinning in the funeral.

But you, children of space, you restless in rest, you shall not be trapped nor tamed. Your house shall be not an anchor but a mast. It shall not be a glistening film that covers a wound, but an eyelid that guards the eye. You shall not fold your wings that you may pass through doors, nor bend your heads that they strike not against a ceiling, nor fear to breathe lest walls should crack and fall down. You shall not dwell in tombs made by the dead for the living. And though of magnificence and splendour, your house shall not hold your secret nor shelter your longing.

For that which is boundless in you abides in the mansion of the sky, whose door is the morning mist, and whose windows are the songs and the silences of night.

# CLOTHES

⸺⫷❈⫸⸺

$A$ND the weaver said, "Speak to us of Clothes."

∽ ∽ ∽

And he answered: Your clothes conceal much of your beauty, yet they hide not the unbeautiful. And though you seek in garments the freedom of privacy you may find in them a harness and a chain. Would that you could meet the sun and the wind with more of your skin and less of your raiment. For the breath of life is in the sunlight and the hand of life is in the wind.

Some of you say, "It is the north wind who has woven the clothes we wear." And I say, Aye, it was the north wind, But shame was his loom, and the softening of the sinews was his thread. And when his work was done he laughed in the forest. Forget not that modesty is for a shield against the eye of the unclean. And when the unclean shall be no more, what were modesty but a fetter and a fouling of the mind?

And forget not that the earth delights to feel your bare feet and the winds long to play with your hair.

# BUYING AND SELLING

AND a merchant said, "Speak to us of Buying and Selling."

And he answered and said: To you the earth yields her fruit, and you shall not want if you but know how to fill your hands. It is in exchanging the gifts of the earth that you shall find abundance and be satisfied. Yet unless the exchange be in love and kindly justice it will but lead some to greed and others to hunger.

When in the market-place you toilers of the sea and fields and vineyards meet the weavers and the potters and the gatherers of spices,—Invoke then the master spirit of the earth, to come into your midst and sanctify the scales and the reckoning that weighs value against value. And suffer not the barren-handed to take part in your transactions, who would sell their words for your labour. To such men you should say: "Come with us to the field, or go with our brothers to the sea and cast your net; For the land and the sea shall be bountiful to you even as to us."

അ‍‍ അ‍‍ അ‍‍

And if there come the singers and the dancers and the flute players,—buy of their gifts also. For they too are gatherers of fruit and frankincense, and that which they bring, though fashioned of dreams, is raiment and food for your soul.

അ‍‍ അ‍‍ അ‍‍

And before you leave the market-place, see that no one has gone his way with empty hands. For the master spirit of the earth shall not sleep peacefully upon the wind till the needs of the least of you are satisfied.

# CRIME AND PUNISHMENT

—————◆━◇━◆—————

$T$HEN one of the judges of the city stood forth and said, "Speak to us of Crime and Punishment."

∽∽ ∽∽ ∽∽

And he answered, saying: It is when your spirit goes wandering upon the wind, That you, alone and unguarded, commit a wrong unto others and therefore unto yourself. And for that wrong committed must you knock and wait a while unheeded at the gate of the blessed.

Like the ocean is your god-self; It remains for ever undefiled. And like the ether it lifts but the winged. Even like the sun is your god-self; It knows not the ways of the mole nor seeks it the holes of the serpent. But your god-self dwells not alone in your being. Much in you is still man, and much in you is not yet man, But a shapeless pigmy that walks asleep in the mist searching for its own awakening. And of the man in you would I now speak.

For it is he and not your god-self nor the pigmy in the mist that knows crime and the punishment of crime.

Oftentimes have I heard you speak of one who commits a wrong as though he were not one of you, but a stranger unto you and an intruder upon your world. But I say that even as the holy and the righteous cannot rise beyond the highest which is in each one of you, So the wicked and the weak cannot fall lower than the lowest which is in you also. And as a single leaf turns not yellow but with the silent knowledge of the whole tree, So the wrong-doer cannot

do wrong without the hidden will of you all.

❦ ❦ ❦

Like a procession you walk together towards your god-self. You are the way and the wayfarers. And when one of you falls down he falls for those behind him, a caution against the stumbling stone.

Aye, and he falls for those ahead of him, who, though faster and surer of foot, yet removed not the stumbling stone.

❦ ❦ ❦

And this also, though the word lie heavy upon your hearts: The murdered is not unaccountable for his own murder, And the robbed is not blameless in being robbed. The righteous is not innocent of the deeds of the wicked, And the white-handed is not clean in the doings of the felon.

❦ ❦ ❦

Yea, the guilty is oftentimes the victim of the injured. And still more often the condemned is the burden bearer for the guiltless and unblamed. You cannot separate the just from the unjust and the good from the wicked; For they stand together before the face of

the sun even as the black thread and the white are woven together.

And when the black thread breaks, the weaver shall look into the whole cloth, and he shall examine the loom also.

If any of you would bring to judgment the unfaithful wife, Let him also weigh the heart of her husband in scales, and measure his soul with measurements. And let him who would lash the offender look unto the spirit of the offended. And if any of you would punish in the name of righteousness and lay the axe unto the evil tree, let him see to its roots; And verily he will find the roots of the good and the bad, the fruitful and the fruitless, all entwined together in the silent heart of the earth.

And you judges who would be just. What judgment pronounce you upon him who though honest in the flesh yet is a thief in spirit? What penalty lay you upon him who slays in the flesh yet is himself slain in the spirit? And how prosecute you him who in action is a deceiver and an oppressor, Yet who also is aggrieved and outraged?

And how shall you punish those whose remorse is already greater than their misdeeds? Is not remorse the justice which is administered by that very law which you would fain serve? Yet you cannot lay remorse upon the innocent nor lift it from the heart of the guilty. Unbidden shall it call in the night, that men may wake and gaze upon themselves. And you who would understand justice, how shall you unless you look upon all deeds in the fullness of light? Only then shall you know that the erect and the fallen are but one man standing in twilight between the night of his pigmy-self and the day of his god self, And that the corner-stone of the temple is not higher than the lowest stone in its foundation.

# LAWS

THEN a lawyer said, "But what of our Laws, master?"

And he answered: You delight in laying down laws, Yet you delight more in breaking them. Like children playing by the ocean who build sand-towers with constancy and then destroy them with laughter. But while you build your sand-towers the ocean brings more sand to the shore, And when you destroy them the ocean laughs with you. Verily the ocean laughs always with the innocent.

But what of those to whom life is not an ocean, and man-made laws are not sand-towers, But to whom life is a rock, and the law a chisel with which they would carve it in their own likeness? What of the cripple who hates dancers? What of the ox who loves his yoke and deems the elk and deer of the forest stray and vagrant things?

∽ ∽ ∽

What of the old serpent who cannot shed his skin, and calls all others naked and shameless? And of him who comes early to the wedding feast, and when over-fed and tired goes his way saying that all feasts are violation and all feasters law-breakers?

∽ ∽ ∽

What shall I say of these save that they too stand in the sunlight, but with their backs to the sun? They see only their shadows, and their shadows are their laws. And what is the sun to them but a caster of shadows? And what is it to acknowledge the laws but to stoop down and trace their shadows upon the earth?

∽ ∽ ∽

But you who walk facing the sun, what images drawn on the

earth can hold you? You who travel with the wind, what weather vane shall direct your course? What man's law shall bind you if you break your yoke but upon no man's prison door? What laws shall you fear if you dance but stumble against no man's iron chains? And who is he that shall bring you to judgment if you tear off your garment yet leave it in no man's path? People of Orphalese, you can muffle the drum, and you can loosen the strings of the lyre, but who shall command the skylark not to sing?

# FREEDOM

꘎꘎꘎

And an orator said, "Speak to us of Freedom."

꘎꘎꘎

And he answered: At the city gate and by your fireside I have seen you prostrate yourself and worship your own freedom, Even as slaves humble themselves before a tyrant and praise him though he slays them. Aye, in the grove of the temple and in the shadow of the citadel I have seen the freest among you wear their freedom as a yoke and a handcuff. And my heart bled within me; for you can only be free when even the desire of seeking freedom becomes a

harness to you, and when you cease to speak of freedom as a goal and a fulfillment. You shall be free indeed when your days are not without a care nor your nights without a want and a grief, But rather when these things girdle your life and yet you rise above them naked and unbound.

ന ന ന

And how shall you rise beyond your days and nights unless you break the chains which you at the dawn of your understanding have fastened around your noon hour? In truth that which you call freedom is the strongest of these chains, though its links glitter in the sun and dazzle your eyes.

ന ന ന

And what is it but fragments of your own self you would discard that you may become free? If it is an unjust law you would abolish, that law was written with your own hand upon your own forehead. You cannot erase it by burning your law books nor by washing the foreheads of your judges, though you pour the sea upon them. And if it is a despot you would dethrone, see first that his throne erected within you is destroyed. For how can a tyrant rule the free and the proud, but for a tyranny in their own freedom and a shame in their

own pride? And if it is a care you would cast off, that care has been chosen by you rather than imposed upon you.

And if it is a fear you would dispel, the seat of that fear is in your heart and not in the hand of the feared. Verily all things move within your being in constant half embrace, the desired and the dreaded, the repugnant and the cherished, the pursued and that which you would escape. These things move within you as lights and shadows in pairs that cling. And when the shadow fades and is no more, the light that lingers becomes a shadow to another light. And thus your freedom when it loses its fetters becomes itself the fetter of a greater freedom.

# REASON AND PASSION

———————⫸⊸⊶⊷⫷———————

AND the priestess spoke again and said: "Speak to us of Reason and Passion."

∽ ∽ ∽

And he answered, saying: Your soul is oftentimes a battlefield, upon which your reason and your judgment wage war against your passion and your appetite. Would that I could be the peacemaker in your soul, that I might turn the discord and the rivalry of your elements into oneness and melody. But how shall I, unless you yourselves be also the peacemakers, nay, the lovers of all your

elements?

တော တော တော

Your reason and your passion are the rudder and the sails of your seafaring soul. If either your sails or your rudder be broken, you can but toss and drift, or else be held at a standstill in mid-seas. For reason, ruling alone, is a force confining; and passion, unattended, is a flame that burns to its own destruction.

တော တော တော

Therefore let your soul exalt your reason to the height of passion, that it may sing; And let it direct your passion with reason, that your passion may live through its own daily resurrection, and like the phoenix rise above its own ashes.

တော တော တော

I would have you consider your judgment and your appetite even as you would two loved guests in your house. Surely you would not honour one guest above the other; for he who is more mindful of one loses the love and the faith of both. Among the hills, when you sit in the cool shade of the white poplars, sharing the peace and serenity of distant fields and meadows—then let your heart

say in silence, "God rests in reason." And when the storm comes, and the mighty wind shakes the forest, and thunder and lightning proclaim the majesty of the sky,—then let your heart say in awe, "God moves in passion." And since you are a breath in God's sphere, and a leaf in God's forest, you too should rest in reason and move in passion.

# PAIN

$\Longrightarrow\!\!\!\!\!\!\!\!\!\Longleftarrow$

$A$ND a woman spoke, saying, "Tell us of Pain."

$\text{\textit{cos cos cos}}$

And he said: Your pain is the breaking of the shell that encloses your understanding. Even as the stone of the fruit must break, that its heart may stand in the sun, so must you know pain. And could you keep your heart in wonder at the daily miracles of your life, your pain would not seem less wondrous than your joy; And you would accept the seasons of your heart, even as you have always accepted the seasons that pass over your fields. And you

would watch with serenity through the winters of your grief. Much of your pain is self-chosen. It is the bitter potion by which the physician within you heals your sick self. Therefore trust the physician, and drink his remedy in silence and tranquillity: For his hand, though heavy and hard, is guided by the tender hand of the Unseen, And the cup he brings, though it burn your lips, has been fashioned of the clay which the Potter has moistened with His own sacred tears.

# SELF-KNOWLEDGE

AND a man said, "Speak to us of Self-Knowledge."

✂⁓ ✂⁓ ✂⁓

And he answered, saying: Your hearts know in silence the secrets of the days and the nights. But your ears thirst for the sound of your heart's knowledge. You would know in words that which you have always known in thought. You would touch with your fingers the naked body of your dreams.

✂⁓ ✂⁓ ✂⁓

And it is well you should. The hidden well-spring of your soul must needs rise and run murmuring to the sea; And the treasure of your infinite depths would be revealed to your eyes. But let there be no scales to weigh your unknown treasure; And seek not the depths of your knowledge with staff or sounding line. For self is a sea boundless and measureless.

Say not, "I have found the truth," but rather, "I have found a truth." Say not, "I have found the path of the soul." Say rather, "I have met the soul walking upon my path." For the soul walks upon all paths. The soul walks not upon a line, neither does it grow like a reed. The soul unfolds itself, like a lotus of countless petals.

# TEACHING

———— ⊹⊙⊱⊙⊹ ————

T HEN said a teacher, "Speak to us of Teaching."

∽ ∽ ∽

And he said: No man can reveal to you aught but that which already lies half asleep in the dawning of your knowledge. The teacher who walks in the shadow of the temple, among his followers, gives not of his wisdom but rather of his faith and his lovingness. If he is indeed wise he does not bid you enter the house of his wisdom, but rather leads you to the threshold of your own mind.

The astronomer may speak to you of his under standing of space, but he cannot give you his under standing. The musician may sing to you of the rhythm which is in all space, but he cannot give you the ear which arrests the rhythm, nor the voice that echoes it. And he who is versed in the science of numbers can tell of the regions of weight and measure, but he cannot conduct you thither.

∽∽∽

For the vision of one man lends not its wings to another man.

And even as each one of you stands alone in God's knowledge, so must each one of you be alone in his knowledge of God and in his under standing of the earth.

# FRIENDSHIP

$\Longleftrightarrow$

$A$ND a youth said, "Speak to us of Friendship."

$\iff$

And he answered, saying: Your friend is your needs answered. He is your field which you sow with love and reap with thanksgiving. And he is your board and your fireside. For you come to him with your hunger, and you seek him for peace.

When your friend speaks his mind you fear not the "nay" in your own mind, nor do you with hold the "aye." And when he is silent

your heart ceases not to listen to his heart; For without words, in friendship, all thoughts, all desires, all expectations are born and shared, with joy that is unclaimed. When you part from your friend, you grieve not; For that which you love most in him may be clearer in his absence, as the mountain to the climber is clearer from the plain. And let there be no purpose in friendship save the deepening of the spirit. For love that seeks aught but the disclosure of its own mystery is not love but a net cast forth: and only the unprofitable is caught.

And let your best be for your friend. If he must know the ebb of your tide, let him know its flood also. For what is your friend that you should seek him with hours to kill? Seek him always with hours to live. For it is his to fill your need, but not your emptiness. And in the sweetness of friendship let there be laughter, and sharing of pleasures. For in the dew of little things the heart finds its morning and is refreshed.

# TALKING

―――――⇥∝✕∝⇤―――――

$A$ND then a scholar said, " Speak of Talking."

∝∞∝ ∝∞∝ ∝∞∝

And he answered, saying: You talk when you cease to be at peace with your thoughts; And when you can no longer dwell in the solitude of your heart you live in your lips, and sound is a diversion and a pastime. And in much of your talking, thinking is half murdered. For thought is a bird of space, that in a cage of words may indeed unfold its wings but cannot fly.

There are those among you who seek the talkative through fear of being alone. The silence of aloneness reveals to their eyes their naked selves and they would escape. And there are those who talk, and without knowledge or forethought reveal a truth which they themselves do not understand. And there are those who have the truth within them, but they tell it not in words. In the bosom of such as these the spirit dwells in rhythmic silence.

When you meet your friend on the roadside or in the market-place, let the spirit in you move your lips and direct your tongue. Let the voice within your voice speak to the ear of his ear; For his soul will keep the truth of your heart as the taste of the wine is remembered. When the colour is forgotten and the vessel is no more.

# TIME

———◁◇▷———

$A$ND an astronomer said, "Master, what of Time?"

∽∽ ∽∽ ∽∽

   And he answered: You would measure time the measureless and the immeasurable. You would adjust your conduct and even direct the course of your spirit according to hours and seasons. Of time you would make a stream upon whose bank you would sit and watch its flowing.

∽∽ ∽∽ ∽∽

Yet the timeless in you is aware of life's timelessness, And knows that yesterday is but today's memory and tomorrow is today's dream. And that which sings and contemplates in you is still dwelling within the bounds of that first moment which scattered the stars into space. Who among you does not feel that his power to love is boundless? And yet who does not feel that very love, though boundless, encompassed within the centre of his being, and moving not from love thought to love thought, nor from love deeds to other love deeds? And is not time even as love is, undivided and paceless?

But if in your thought you must measure time into seasons, let each season encircle all the other seasons, And let today embrace the past with remembrance and the future with longing.

# GOOD AND EVIL

$A$ND one of the elders of the city said, "Speak to us of Good and Evil."

And he answered: Of the good in you I can speak, but not of the evil. For what is evil but good tortured by its own hunger and thirst? Verily when good is hungry it seeks food even in dark caves, and when it thirsts it drinks even of dead waters.

You are good when you are one with yourself. Yet when you are not one with yourself you are not evil. For a divided house is not a den of thieves; it is only a divided house. And a ship without rudder may wander aimlessly among perilous isles yet sink not to the bottom.

⁓ ⁓ ⁓

You are good when you strive to give of yourself. Yet you are not evil when you seek gain for yourself. For when you strive for gain you are but a root that clings to the earth and sucks at her breast. Surely the fruit cannot say to the root, "Be like me, ripe and full and ever giving of your abundance." For to the fruit giving is a need, as receiving is a need to the root.

⁓ ⁓ ⁓

You are good when you are fully awake in your speech. Yet you are not evil when you sleep while your tongue staggers without purpose. And even stumbling speech may strengthen a weak tongue.

⁓ ⁓ ⁓

You are good when you walk to your goal firmly and with bold

steps. Yet you are not evil when you go thither limping. Even those who limp go not backward. But you who are strong and swift, see that you do not limp before the lame, deeming it kindness.

cరు cరు cరు

You are good in countless ways, and you are not evil when you are not good, You are only loitering and sluggard. Pity that the stags cannot teach swiftness to the turtles.

cరు cరు cరు

In your longing for your giant self lies your goodness: and that longing is in all of you. But in some of you that longing is a torrent rushing with might to the sea, carrying the secrets of the hillsides and the songs of the forest. And in others it is a flat stream that loses itself in angles and bends and lingers before it reaches the shore. But let not him who longs much say to him who longs little, "Wherefore are you slow and halting?" For the truly good ask not the naked, "Where is your garment?" nor the houseless, "What has befallen your house?"

# PRAYER

⸺⟡⸺

THEN a priestess said, "Speak to us of Prayer."

∽ ∽ ∽

And he answered, saying: You pray in your distress and in your need; would that you might pray also in the fullness of your joy and in your days of abundance.

∽ ∽ ∽

For what is prayer but the expansion of your self into the living ether? And if it is for your comfort to pour your darkness into

space, it is also for your delight to pour forth the dawning of your heart. And if you cannot but weep when your soul summons you to prayer, she should spur you again and yet again, though weeping, until you shall come laughing.

∽∽∽

When you pray you rise to meet in the air those who are praying at that very hour, and whom save in prayer you may not meet. Therefore let your visit to that temple invisible be for naught but ecstasy and sweet communion. For if you should enter the temple for no other purpose than asking you shall not receive: And if you should enter into it to humble yourself you shall not be lifted: Or even if you should enter into it to beg for the good of others you shall not be heard. It is enough that you enter the temple invisible.

∽∽∽

I cannot teach you how to pray in words. God listens not to your words save when He Himself utters them through your lips. And I cannot teach you the prayer of the seas and the forests and the mountains. But you who are born of the mountains and the forests and the seas can find their prayer in your heart, And if you but listen in the stillness of the night you shall hear them saying in

silence: Our God, who art our winged self, it is thy will in us that willeth. "It is thy desire in us that desireth. "It is thy urge in us that would turn our nights, which are thine, into days, which are thine also.

"We cannot ask thee for aught, for thou knowest our needs before they are born in us:

"Thou art our need; and in giving us more of thyself thou givest us all."

# PLEASURE

THEN a hermit, who visited the city once a year, came forth and said, "Speak to us of Pleasure."

And he answered, saying: Pleasure is a freedom-song, But it is not freedom. It is the blossoming of your desires, But it is not their fruit. It is a depth calling unto a height, But it is not the deep nor the high. It is the caged taking wing, But it is not space encompassed. Aye, in very truth, pleasure is a freedom-song. And I fain would have you sing it with fullness of heart; yet I would not

have you lose your hearts in the singing.

က္ကာ က္ကာ

Some of your youth seek pleasure as if it were all, and they are judged and rebuked. I would not judge nor rebuke them. I would have them seek. For they shall find pleasure, but not her alone;

Seven are her sisters, and the least of them is more beautiful than pleasure. Have you not heard of the man who was digging in the earth for roots and found a treasure?

က္ကာ က္ကာ

And some of your elders remember pleasures with regret like wrongs committed in drunkenness. But regret is the beclouding of the mind and not its chastisement. They should remember their pleasures with gratitude, as they would the harvest of a summer. Yet if it comforts them to regret, let them be comforted.

က္ကာ က္ကာ

And there are among you those who are neither young to seek nor old to remember; And in their fear of seeking and remembering they shun all pleasures, lest they neglect the spirit or offend against

it. But even in their foregoing is their pleasure. And thus they too find a treasure though they dig for roots with quivering hands.

∽ ∽ ∽

But tell me, who is he that can offend the spirit? Shall the nightingale offend the stillness of the night, or the firefly the stars? And shall your flame or your smoke burden the wind? Think you the spirit is a still pool which you can trouble with a staff?

∽ ∽ ∽

Oftentimes in denying yourself pleasure you do but store the desire in the recesses of your being. Who knows but that which seems omitted to day, waits for tomorrow? Even your body knows its heritage and its rightful need and will not be deceived. And your body is the harp of your soul, And it is yours to bring forth sweet music from it or confused sounds.

∽ ∽ ∽

And now you ask in your heart, "How shall we distinguish that which is good in pleasure from that which is not good?" Go to your fields and your gardens, and you shall learn that it is the pleasure of the bee to gather honey of the flower, But it is also the

pleasure of the flower to yield its honey to the bee. For to the bee a flower is a fountain of life, And to the flower a bee is a messenger of love, And to both, bee and flower, the giving and the receiving of pleasure is a need and an ecstasy.

People of Orphalese, be in your pleasures like the flowers and the bees.

# BEAUTY

⤙⬦⤚

AND a poet said, "Speak to us of Beauty."

⟋⟍ ⟋⟍ ⟋⟍

And he answered: Where shall you seek beauty, and how shall you find her unless she herself be your way and your guide? And how shall you speak of her except she be the weaver of your speech?

⟋⟍ ⟋⟍ ⟋⟍

The aggrieved and the injured say, "Beauty is kind and gentle.

Like a young mother half-shy of her own glory she walks among us." And the passionate say, "Nay, beauty is a thing of might and dread. Like the tempest she shakes the earth beneath us and the sky above us."

∽∽∽

The tired and the weary say, "Beauty is of soft whisperings. She speaks in our spirit. Her voice yields to our silences like a faint light that quivers in fear of the shadow." But the restless say, "We have heard her shouting among the mountains, And with her cries came the sound of hoofs, and the beating of wings and the roaring of lions."

∽∽∽

At night the watchmen of the city say, "Beauty shall rise with the dawn from the east." And at noontide the toilers and the wayfarers say, "We have seen her leaning over the earth from the windows of the sunset."

∽∽∽

In winter say the snow-bound, "She shall come with the spring leaping upon the hills." And in the summer heat the reapers say, "We

have seen her dancing with the autumn leaves, and we saw a drift of snow in her hair." All these things have you said of beauty, Yet in truth you spoke not of her but of needs unsatisfied, And beauty is not a need but an ecstasy.

⤫ ⤫ ⤫

It is not a mouth thirsting nor an empty hand stretched forth, But rather a heart inflamed and a soul enchanted. It is not the image you would see nor the song you would hear, But rather an image you see though you close your eyes and a song you hear though you shut your ears. It is not the sap within the furrowed bark, nor a wing attached to a claw, But rather a garden for ever in bloom and a flock of angels for ever in flight.

⤫ ⤫ ⤫

People of Orphalese, beauty is life when life unveils her holy face. But you are life and you are the veil. Beauty is eternity gazing at itself in a mirror. But you are eternity and you are the mirror.

# RELIGION

———— ⪦⪧⪖⪕ ————

$A$ND an old priest said, "Speak to us of Religion."

⪦⪧ ⪦⪧ ⪦⪧

And he said: Have I spoken this day of aught else? Is not religion all deeds and all reflection, And that which is neither deed nor reflection, but a wonder and a surprise ever springing in the soul, even while the hands hew the stone or tend the loom?

⪦⪧ ⪦⪧ ⪦⪧

Who can separate his faith from his actions, or his belief from

his occupations? Who can spread his hours before him, saying, "This for God and this for myself; This for my soul and this other for my body"?

❦ ❦ ❦

All your hours are wings that beat through space from self to self. He who wears his morality but as his best garment were better naked. The wind and the sun will tear no holes in his skin. And he who defines his conduct by ethics imprisons his song-bird in a cage. The freest song comes not through bars and wires.

❦ ❦ ❦

And he to whom worshipping is a window, to open but also to shut, has not yet visited the house of his soul whose windows are from dawn to dawn.

❦ ❦ ❦

Your daily life is your temple and your religion. Whenever you enter into it take with you your all. Take the plough and the forge and the mallet and the lute, The things you have fashioned in necessity or for delight. For in reverie you cannot rise above your achievements nor fall lower than your failures. And take with you

all men: For in adoration you cannot fly higher than their hopes nor humble yourself lower than their despair.

And if you would know God, be not therefore a solver of riddles. Rather look about you and you shall see Him playing with your children. And look into space; you shall see Him walking in the cloud, outstretching His arms in the lightning and descending in rain. You shall see Him smiling in flowers, then rising and waving His hands in trees.

# DEATH

―――――◦◦◦――――――

THEN Almitra spoke, saying, "We would ask now of Death."

◦◦ ◦◦ ◦◦

And he said: You would know the secret of death. But how shall you find it unless you seek it in the heart of life? The owl whose night-bound eyes are blind unto the day cannot unveil the mystery of light. If you would indeed behold the spirit of death, open your heart wide unto the body of life. For life and death are one, even as the river and the sea are one.

In the depth of your hopes and desires lies your silent knowledge of the beyond; And like seeds dreaming beneath the snow your heart dreams of spring. Trust the dreams, for in them is hidden the gate to eternity.

Your fear of death is but the trembling of the shepherd when he stands before the king whose hand is to be laid upon him in honour. Is the shepherd not joyful beneath his trembling, that he shall wear the mark of the king? Yet is he not more mindful of his trembling?

∽ ∽ ∽

For what is it to die but to stand naked in the wind and to melt into the sun? And what is it to cease breathing but to free the breath from its restless tides, that it may rise and expand and seek God unencumbered?

∽ ∽ ∽

Only when you drink from the river of silence shall you indeed sing. And when you have reached the mountain top, then you shall begin to climb. And when the earth shall claim your limbs, then shall you truly dance.

## THE FAREWELL

$\multimap\!\!\diamond\!\!\multimap$

$A$ND now it was evening.

And Almitra the seeress said, "Blessed be this day and this place and your spirit that has spoken."

And he answered, Was it I who spoke? Was I not also a listener?

$\infty$ $\infty$ $\infty$

Then he descended the steps of the Temple and all the people followed him. And he reached his ship and stood upon the deck.

And facing the people again, he raised his voice and said:

People of Orphalese, the wind bids me leave you. Less hasty am I than the wind, yet I must go. We wanderers, ever seeking the lonelier way, begin no day where we have ended another day; and no sunrise finds us where sunset left us. Even while the earth sleeps we travel. We are the seeds of the tenacious plant, and it is in our ripeness and our fullness of heart that we are given to the wind and are scattered.

Brief were my days among you, and briefer still the words I have spoken. But should my voice fade in your ears, and my love vanish in your memory, then I will come again, And with a richer heart and lips more yielding to the spirit will I speak. Yea, I shall return with the tide, And though death may hide me, and the greater silence enfold me, yet again will I seek your under standing. And not in vain will I seek. If aught I have said is truth, that truth shall reveal itself in a clearer voice, and in words more kin to your thoughts.

I go with the wind, people of Orphalese, but not down into emptiness; And if this day is not a fulfillment of your needs and my love, then let it be a promise till another day. Man's needs change, but not his love, nor his desire that his love should satisfy his needs. Know, therefore, that from the greater silence I shall return.

The mist that drifts away at dawn, leaving but dew in the fields, shall rise and gather into a cloud and then fall down in rain. And not unlike the mist have I been. In the stillness of the night I have walked in your streets, and my spirit has entered your houses, And your heart-beats were in my heart, and your breath was upon my face, and I knew you all.

Aye, I knew your joy and your pain, and in your sleep your dreams were my dreams. And oftentimes I was among you a lake among the mountains. I mirrored the summits in you and the bending slopes, and even the passing flocks of your thoughts and your desires. And to my silence came the laughter of your children in streams, and the longing of your youths in rivers. And when they reached my depth the streams and the rivers ceased not yet to

sing. But sweeter still than laughter and greater than longing came to me.

It was the boundless in you; The vast man in whom you are all but cells and sinews; He in whose chant all your singing is but a soundless throbbing. It is in the vast man that you are vast, And in beholding him that I beheld you and loved you. For what distances can love reach that are not in that vast sphere? What visions, what expectations and what presumptions can outsoar that flight? Like a giant oak tree covered with apple blossoms is the vast man in you. His might binds you to the earth, his fragrance lifts you into space, and in his durability you are deathless.

You have been told that, even like a chain, you are as weak as your weakest link. This is but half the truth. You are also as strong as your strongest link. To measure you by your smallest deed is to reckon the power of ocean by the frailty of its foam. To judge you by your failures is to cast blame upon the seasons for their inconstancy.

Aye, you are like an ocean, And though heavy-grounded ships await the tide upon your shores, yet, even like an ocean, you cannot hasten your tides. And like the seasons you are also, And though in your winter you deny your spring, Yet spring, reposing within you, smiles in her drowsiness and is not offended.

Think not I say these things in order that you may say the one to the other, "He praised us well. He saw but the good in us." I only speak to you in words of that which you yourselves know in thought. And what is word knowledge but a shadow of wordless knowledge? Your thoughts and my words are waves from a sealed memory that keeps records of our yesterdays, And of the ancient days when the earth knew not us nor herself, And of nights when earth was upwrought with confusion.

Wise men have come to you to give you of their wisdom. I came to take of your wisdom: And behold I have found that which is greater than wisdom. It is a flame spirit in you ever gathering more of itself, While you, heedless of its expansion, bewail the withering

of your days. It is life in quest of life in bodies that fear the grave.

*ಲ್ಲ ಲ್ಲ ಲ್ಲ*

There are no graves here. These mountains and plains are a cradle and a stepping-stone. Whenever you pass by the field where you have laid your ancestors look well thereupon, and you shall see yourselves and your children dancing hand in hand. Verily you often make merry without knowing.

*ಲ್ಲ ಲ್ಲ ಲ್ಲ*

Others have come to you to whom for golden promises made unto you faith you have given but riches and power and glory. Less than a promise have I given, and yet more generous have you been to me. You have given me my deeper thirsting after life. Surely there is no greater gift to a man than that which turns all his aims into parching lips and all life into a fountain. And in this lies my honour and my reward,—That whenever I come to the fountain to drink I find the living water itself thirsty; And it drinks me while I drink it.

Some of you have deemed me proud and over shy to receive gifts. Too proud indeed am I to receive wages, but not gifts. And

though I have eaten berries among the hills when you would have had me sit at your board, And slept in the portico of the temple when you would gladly have sheltered me, Yet it was not your loving mindfulness of my days and my nights that made food sweet to my mouth and girdled my sleep with visions?

For this I bless you most: You give much and know not that you give at all. Verily the kindness that gazes upon itself in a mirror turns to stone, And a good deed that calls itself by tender names becomes the parent to a curse.

And some of you have called me aloof, and drunk with my own aloneness, And you have said, "He holds council with the trees of the forest, but not with men. "He sits alone on hill-tops and looks down upon our city." True it is that I have climbed the hills and walked in remote places. How could I have seen you save from a great height or a great distance? How can one be indeed near unless he be far?

And others among you called unto me, not in words, and they

said: "Stranger, stranger, lover of unreachable heights, why dwell you among the summits where eagles build their nests? Why seek you the unattainable? What storms would you trap in your net, and what vaporous birds do you hunt in the sky? Come and be one of us. Descend and appease your hunger with our bread and quench your thirst with our wine."

In the solitude of their souls they said these things; But were their solitude deeper they would have known that I sought but the secret of your joy and your pain, And I hunted only your larger selves that walk the sky. But the hunter was also the hunted; For many of my arrows left my bow only to seek my own breast. And the flier was also the creeper; For when my wings were spread in the sun their shadow upon the earth was a turtle. And I the believer was also the doubter; For often have I put my finger in my own wound that I might have the greater belief in you and the greater knowledge of you.

And it is with this belief and this knowledge that I say, You are not enclosed within your bodies, nor confined to houses or fields. That which is you dwells above the mountain and roves with

the wind. It is not a thing that crawls into the sun for warmth or digs holes into darkness for safety, But a thing free, a spirit that envelops the earth and moves in the ether.

If these be vague words, then seek not to clear them. Vague and nebulous is the beginning of all things, but not their end, And I fain would have you remember me as a beginning. Life, and all that lives, is conceived in the mist and not in the crystal. And who knows but a crystal is mist in decay?

This would I have you remember in remembering me: That which seems most feeble and bewildered in you is the strongest and most determined. Is it not your breath that has erected and hardened the structure of your bones? And is it not a dream which none of you re member having dreamt, that built your city and fashioned all there is in it? Could you but see the tides of that breath you would cease to see all else, And if you could hear the whispering of the dream you would hear no other sound.

But you do not see, nor do you hear, and it is well. The veil that clouds your eyes shall be lifted by the hands that wove it, And the clay that fills your ears shall be pierced by those fingers that kneaded it. And you shall see. And you shall hear. Yet you shall not deplore having known blindness, nor regret having been deaf. For in that day you shall know the hidden purposes in all things, And you shall bless darkness as you would bless light.

After saying these things he looked about him, and he saw the pilot of his ship standing by the helm and gazing now at the full sails and now at the distance.

And he said: Patient, over patient, is the captain of my ship. The wind blows, and restless are the sails; Even the rudder begs direction; Yet quietly my captain awaits my silence. And these my mariners, who have heard the choir of the greater sea, they too have heard me patiently. Now they shall wait no longer. I am ready. The stream has reached the sea, and once more the great mother holds her son against her breast.

Fare you well, people of Orphalese. This day has ended. It is closing upon us even as the water-lily upon its own tomorrow. What was given us here we shall keep, And if it suffices not, then again must we come together and together stretch our hands unto the giver. Forget not that I shall come back to you. A little while, and my longing shall gather dust and foam for another body. A little while, a moment of rest upon the wind, and another woman shall bear me.

Farewell to you and the youth I have spent with you. It was but yesterday we met in a dream. You have sung to me in my aloneness, and I of your longings have built a tower in the sky. But now our sleep has fled and our dream is over, and it is no longer dawn.

The noontide is upon us and our half waking has turned to fuller day, and we must part. If in the twilight of memory we should meet once more, we shall speak again together and you shall sing to me a deeper song. And if our hands should meet in another dream we shall build another tower in the sky.

So saying he made a signal to the seamen, and straightaway they weighed anchor and cast the ship loose from its moorings, and they moved eastward. And a cry came from the people as from a single heart, and it rose into the dusk and was carried out over the sea like a great trumpeting. Only Almitra was silent, gazing after the ship until it had vanished into the mist. And when all the people were dispersed she still stood alone upon the sea-wall, remembering in her heart his saying:

"A little while, a moment of rest upon the wind, and another woman shall bear me."